Nolin smiled crookedly, nodded and left the engine room.

His knowledge of the shift engine was limited but greater than anyone else's aboard ship except for Barse. Likewise, he knew more about each system than anyone but the officer in charge.

He couldn't operate the weapons computer with Sarov's flair, but he could keep the ship from being destroyed. His abilities in life support matched Liottey's — he had been in training for executive officer before deciding command pilot suited him better.

Of all the positions, he knew the least about what it took to work Chikako Miza's station. He vowed to bone up on communications and detection. With Pensky in charge, he would have the spare time.

He slid through the shielding baffles leading to the bridge and stopped just inside the hatch. Pandemonium reigned. It took him several seconds to understand that the *Preceptor* was at full battle alert — and that Mitri Sarov worked to load missiles for firing.

"Who's attacking? The Death Fleet?" he called across to Miza. She shook her head. He had never seen her so pale.

"Please, Captain Pensky," she pleaded. "It is giving all the proper recognition signals. It's one of ours!"

ALSO BY

Robert E. Vardeman

STAR FRONTIERS

Alien Death Fleet
The Genetic Menace

AFTER THE SPELL WARS

Ogre Castle
In The Sea Nymph's Lair

STAR FRONTIERS 1

ALIEN DEATH FLEET

ROBERT E. VARDEMAN

ZUMAYA OTHERWORLDS   AUSTIN TX

2008

This book is a work of fiction. Names, characters, places and incidents are products of the author's imagination or are used fictitiously. Any resemblance to actual persons or events is purely coincidental.

ALIEN DEATH FLEET
© 2008 by Robert E. Vardeman
ISBN: 978-1-934135-83-9
Cover art © Brad Foster
Cover design © Martine Jardin & Tamian Wood

Zumaya Otherworlds is an imprint of Zumaya Publications LLC, Austin, Texas.

Library of Congress Cataloging-in-Publication Data

Vardeman, Robert E.
  Alien death fleet / by Robert E. Vardeman.
     p. cm. -- (Star frontiers ; 1)
  ISBN 978-1-934135-83-9 (alk. paper)
  1. Space ships--Fiction. I. Title.
  PS3572.A714A79 2008
  813'.54--dc22
                                        2008007372

For Patty. Who else?

Chapter One

Assistant Far Space Controller Blenn stirred and came awake slowly in the comfortable command chair. For several seconds, he could not separate dream from the reality of the heads-up display all around him. The dream had been nice, so nice. He slipped back into the dream and smiled as he recalled the way he and the fine, willing, dark-haired Lola from the robo-maintenance department had used her telepresence controllers to—

Blenn snapped fully alert when the warning gong sounded. He almost fell from his chair in his haste to bring up the full probe screens showing the outer fringe of the system. Never in the three months he had been on duty in this sector had anything more interesting than a small asteroid appeared. Even that worthless hunk of rock and water ice had been even more boring than usual.

Dozens of new red lights blossomed like madness in Blenn's HUD, almost blinding him. He blinked most of them off. Even at minimal display, too many flashing lights remained for it to be anything but a malfunction.

"Damned incompetents," he grumbled as he leaned forward to manually cancel what had to be spurious readings from his control board. "Nobody can repair anything right anymore. Whatever happened to good maintenance programmers?"

His anger faded and his heart threatened to run away when he discovered a fully operational board. A second check returned the identical results. Functional board, disaster imminent.

He leaned back for a moment, barely understanding the magnitude of his problem. Then, as he overcame his shock, he spun and hit the big blue supervisor alert button.

"Danil, I've got a thousand indications of penetration. It must be a comet that split apart. But what a comet!" His gaze flashed to the mass detectors incrementing at the side of his HUD. He turned cold all over when he saw the densitometer readings. This was no gaseous, half-frozen ball of ammonia that had split apart. Quick eye movements got the computer to analyzing the data. Transuranic elements. The exact isotopes used in FTL shift engines.

He had detected a fleet of more than ten thousand vessels.

"Show me. Transfer to my board. I'm not getting anything," came the supervisor's irritable voice. Danil, too, had been disturbed and did not appreciate it. He hadn't been dreaming of Lola; he had been with her.

"Why can't you see it? It should have lit every board in the center."

The far-space controller fought to keep from shouting. He settled down and tried to think it through. Danil grumbled constantly, even after the readings transferred to his HUD.

"You're demoted one rank," snapped Danil. "There's nothing unusual on the readouts. Quit daydreaming on duty."

"But. . . " Blenn fell silent. All indication of an invasion fleet had winked off his densitometer and mass spectrometer readouts. He leaned back, sweating in spite of the cool wind blowing from the small room's air ducts.

He had done the preliminary checks and his equipment functioned within design parameters.

"Damned if I know what's going on," Blenn said to himself. He began working through a full systems check. Fifty seconds later, he stabbed his finger down on the supervisor's call button again.

"What is it now?"

"The peripherals are malfunctioning. Run your own check. Something has circumvented them."

"Impossible. That would take weeks of work, even if someone knew where all the detectors orbited. Not even the damned rebels could spend the time doing that without being discovered."

"Someone did it—and they were a fraction of a minute off in cutting in their own readings. We're getting recordings, not real-time pickup."

The irascible supervisor cursed, then chased Lola from his office and began his own circuitry check. The expression on his face gradually changed from irritation to disbelief. Then he turned and alerted his own superior.

Assistant Far Space Controller Blenn relaxed. He had done all he could to warn of possible trouble. He remained unsure what had occurred, but he knew heads would roll somewhere. If it happened to be Danil, fine. The way he eyed Lola made Blenn a trifle uneasy. He leaned back, knowing he had done all he could.

Still, something unusual was happening, and it made him uneasy.

He remained unsure until the Death Fleet appeared in formation at a range close enough to rake his home planet with their radiation cannons.

* * *

The boy should have been in school, but the afternoon was too warm to endure another instant of stuffy classroom. He had not bothered returning to his school console; it might be an hour before a random check showed he wasn't working.

He leaned back in the center of the grassy meadow, head resting on his folded hands. He had plugged in an old math drill program he had finished weeks ago. Computer teachers were so dumb sometimes.

Not that he minded. The warm air turned him drowsy, and the few breezes blowing up from the valley carried a hint of rain that might fall later. He remembered distant Earth with no real pleasure. The weather there was too predictable. Anyone could vote on what they wanted. It seldom rained because everyone insisted on sunshine.

He liked occasional rain. It made him feel...sinful. That was the only way he could describe it. He wasn't supposed to get wet. His clothing disintegrated, and his mother had to reprogram and use precious ration units, but he didn't care.

He liked the feel of rain against his face.

He drifted, more asleep than awake.

The roar, like a million thunderclaps, brought him bolt upright. His eyes widened as he stared at the cloud-specked turquoise sky. Huge patches of festering black appeared everywhere. At first, he thought it might be storm clouds forming. Then he caught the glint of sunlight off flat black metal.

"Ships," he whispered, as if someone might overhear. "There must be a million of them up there."

There were only ten thousand, but they worked in perfect coordination and performed the deadly work of orders of magnitudes more.

The boy grinned when he saw a rainbow arch down from a black ship. It was so gentle, so peaceful, such a promise of rain and freedom and everything he enjoyed so.

The grin faded when he realized that the bright rainbow did not bring assurance but death. Anything living within the path of the rapidly sweeping shaft of radiant energy died horribly.

He shot to his feet when he saw the blackened grass appear at the edge of the meadow. A tree exploded and spewed boiling sap in all directions; the burned-out carcass looked like a flailing black skeleton. One finger pointed at him, marking him for death.

He didn't bother putting on his boots. Barefoot, he ran for his life, crushed grass wetly staining his feet.

The swathe of death followed — too fast.

He never saw the lovely rainbow. The ionizing radiation from the warship burst apart every cell in his body. He experienced a surge of pain and then infinite blackness and death possessed him.

The rainbow scoured the meadow of all life and swept on, seeking anything living and leaving undisturbed all inanimate objects.

❆ ❆ ❆

"They might as well be saturation bombing with neutron bombs," the scoutship pilot told his three passengers. They crowded into a space cramped with only two.

The pilot had been preparing to lift when the enemy ships struck. He and three maintenance men had launched into a low-planet orbit, escaping the first delicate and deadly rainbow touch by seconds.

"You mean they're not blowing up anything? They're just killing anything alive?"

"Looks like," the pilot said. He worked on his small vidscreen. He made contact with a dozen checkpoints, but no human responded. All automated transponders worked without a glitch, but the living controllers behind them did not answer.

Using both his optical detection and synthetic-aperture radar mapping equipment, he watched the progress of the destruction below. He felt like vomiting. Cities that had teemed with people now stood devoid of life. It looked as if the inhabitants had simply left, but he knew they were slumped over consoles and in lobbies and in transit equipment, fried beyond recognition. The rainbow weapon had not cared if they were newborn or old; all died under its implacable caress.

"Why didn't we have any warning? Those bastards in Far Space Control must have sold us out!" The maintenance man raged and tried to swing his fist. The compartment was too cramped. The two beside him restrained him from further angry outbursts.

"The controllers? I doubt it. Why let in a fleet that's not likely to take any prisoners? That…That's a death fleet!"

"They sold us out. What other explanation can there be?"

The pilot shrugged. He had no idea. He worked mapping the rocky outer planets in the system. Occasionally, he sent small detectors speeding on their way into orbit around the primary. Ever since Mordred III had been devastated by the comet, all Earther colonies kept close watch for incoming cometary objects. A fleet this large could not have slipped by unseen.

"They might have burned out the detectors," suggested another. "You know they're easy targets for proton storms."

"If all the detectors went out simultaneously, there'd still be an alert. We got nothing. And why didn't someone spot such a huge fleet on radar? There's continuous scanning to keep our near-planet traffic under control."

"Good questions," the pilot said, his gorge rising as he watched the efficient death meted out to his home world by the stark, black-metal-hulled fleet. He switched on all his recorders and got what information he could on the ships and their weapons. He knew it was pitifully small and insignificant. A combat scout might have discovered more. A combat scout might have also been destroyed.

Death Fleet. He grimly let the name roll over and over in his head. It was fitting. Too fitting for comfort—or survival.

The pilot checked his energy leakage. The tiny scout might have been dead in space for all the power it consumed. Most of the power required went for air circulation and purification. He kept the engines on standby and used only minimal capacity for the radar spying.

He closed his eyes and rubbed them. Spying. That's what this was. An enemy had swept through the system and unerringly found the nerve center for the planet. He had seen the way the rainbow energy weapons sought out the defensive positions, the military complex, the places around the city where ships might be launched to defend a hapless world. He had been lucky, ready to launch, engines hot. Taking on his passengers had been unexpected but necessary, seeing the radiation weapon from the Death Fleet working its way across the launch facility.

He rubbed his eyes even harder. The heat inside the ship from the four bodies overwhelmed the small exchanger unit's capacity. Already, the air tasted stale and laden with sweat and fear. Was he really lucky?

"What are they doing now?" one of the men demanded.

"They're systematically beaming the surface," the pilot said. "There's no way anyone will be left alive."

"Bastards."

"Who are they?" asked another. "This isn't some rebel group out to overthrow the Empire."

The pilot shook his head wearily. What did it matter? He doubted rebels had the support to build the immense fleet now orbiting the planet. If they did, they would directly attack the Emperor on Earth. His own sympathies lay with the rebels rather than the genetically altered Emperor, but those were distant concerns now. He enjoyed living on the frontier, as primitive as it was, because he didn't have to think about the strutting, prancing, superior men and women and other genetically enhanced…things. Here, he did his job and everyone — every human — left him alone.

Everyone except the people in huge black spaceships with radiation weapons efficiently killing every human on the planet.

He scowled when he saw a few hundred of the largest ships change position into polar orbits with exaggerated eccentricity. He punched the data into his onboard computer.

The ships maneuvered to give them the most time low over the major land masses. The pilot watched in fascination as the first of the immense ships dipped down and looked as if it fell apart.

"They blew up!" cried a man, peering over his shoulder.

"No," the pilot said, thinking furiously. He worked on the computer, making sure he recorded every instant of the strange operation. "They're landing. They're actually invading the planet."

"All the Empire Service tactical officers say that's not possible."

"They're doing it." The pilot increased magnification and watched as massive land rovers spread out.

"What *are* they doing?" asked another.

"Can't say, but it might be that they're looting the planet." The pilot shifted the memory blocks from his mapping cameras into a radiation-shielded safety vault then cycled in new cerampix to record every detail. "They used their radiation weapons to scour the planet of life. They want what's left."

"They're welcome to my vidset," grumbled the third man, who had been silent to this point. "Damned thing never worked right."

The pilot tried to make sense of what he saw. Until he had seen the efficient dark automated beetles moving out to scoop up the spoils of genocide, he had considered the remote possibility that rebels really were behind the attack. No rebel needed the types of materiel disappearing into the automated maws below.

"Aliens," he muttered. "I'd heard rumors of a couple systems getting hit, but I thought it was all outgassing."

"I heard something similar in a bar. The Proteus, down by Jeffcan Supply? You know the place?"

The pilot grunted noncommittally. The man rattled on about how a drunken coworker had told him of major destruction wrought farther out in the Orion Arm.

"We've got to get to another system. They took us by surprise. I don't know how, but they did. We can stop them. Look at those ships. There's not a one that can stand up to an Empire Service cruiser. They seem all fragile and… I don't know. Diffuse? But they're big bastards. All we need is time to prepare."

"So how are we going to do it? I'm getting damned hot in here. Can't you turn up the heat pump on this tub?"

The other maintenance men grumbled about the rising temperature, too. The pilot didn't bother telling them the scoutship was at the limits of its operational capacity already. They worked on ships similar to his every day and knew the workings better than he ever could. They complained only to assure themselves something was right in the universe.

For his own part, he wasn't sure. He couldn't take his eyes off the magnified image on his vidscreen showing the huge automated pirate factories below reducing a planet's wealth to easily looted crates. The beetle-shaped machines rolled forward, devouring everything in front of them, then excreted their fodder in a long trail behind. He shifted his view and saw new machines being dropped by other ships. These machines scooped up the crates and jetted upward immediately. He guessed the process would go on endlessly until everything the Death Fleet wanted was stripped from the world.

The Death Fleet. He screwed his eyes closed and tried to force the name from his brain. It was not possible because it was too descriptive.

"They've finished bombarding the planet," the pilot said, a hollowness rising inside. That meant nothing survived below—except the alien looters. He didn't have a family to speak of on-planet, and he had just broken up with his girlfriend, but they were all dead now. His boss and the few friends he had made and even the most casual acquaintances—all gone. Dead.

Dead by alien hand. Neither the black ships nor the automated looting factories were anything he had ever seen before. To his way of thinking that meant aliens.

His knuckles turned white as he clutched hard at the edge of the control panel. A strong hand on his shoulder brought him out of his emotional wasteland of loss and anger.

"What?" he snapped.

"We got to do something. We're not outfitted for a long trip, not with four of us aboard. There's nothing for any of us down there." The maintenance man pointed toward the vidscreen showing the voracious black beetle machines creeping through the city, tiny robot feeders scurrying back and forth to keep a steady flow through the packager. Crates dropped behind the machine and were hurried to cleared areas where the ferries swooped down for them.

"They've done this before," he said, anger rising. "This isn't the first world they're destroyed and robbed. They're too efficient for this to be new to them."

"Space take 'em," the man said. "The world's gone. The whole damned colony has bought it. We've got to think about our own necks."

"We can't shift for another system. There's too much mass and not enough fuel for that." The pilot laughed harshly. "There's not even enough oxygen, and we'd fry halfway there. It's harder to get rid of waste heat in shift space than it is in normal space."

"How many can this wreck shift safely?" the man asked in a low voice.

"Two. Maybe three, but that's pushing back the bubble's edge. Why do you...?"

The pilot watched with a growing sickness as the man swung around. A short punch with the tips of his fingers crushed one man's windpipe. Before the third maintenance man could respond, his met the same fate. Both had been killed with a minimum of fuss or mess.

"We'd better waste the air and jettison them. I don't want to share the compartment with two dead men all the way to...where?"

The brightness in the killer's eyes made the pilot stammer. "Nearest planet. Lyman IV. Yes, Lyman IV."

❋ ❋ ❋

The two bodies drifted just outside the scoutship. The pilot couldn't take his eyes off the near-view vidscreen showing hull conditions. The dead faces always seemed to swing around toward him, open and accusing eyes fixed on him.

He began laying in a course through shift space — the only reason he still lived. The maintenance man could kill him any time, but he needed piloting expertise. One vidscreen filled with two dead bodies and another showing massive plundering, the pilot set the computer for the shift.

He wondered how long he would live.

He wondered how long any human would.

Chapter Two

Pier Norlin stretched and yawned. Picket ship duty was dreary. Being stuck in a long apogee orbit required a duty tour of more than three months with little to do. The automated equipment recorded a vast array of data for a half-dozen different scientific studies. Most of it Sub-Lieutenant Norlin ignored, except to service if necessary—and it seldom was. The equipment had been well designed and required very little maintenance.

Some of it he tended as if it meant the world to him, because it accumulated data for a PhD candidate, Neela Cosarrian. He had listened endlessly to her telling what the equipment did and what she expected to discover, relating to her degree in multi-dimensional membrane physics. He had only a vague idea what it all meant, but he could listen endlessly to the petite scientist describe her research. He had done well at Empire Service Academy on Sutton II before assignment in the Lyman IV system as a research adjunct, but his specialty field had been electronics and command, not physics and analysis.

That did not bother Neela at all. Too many other academics looked askance at a lowly sub-lieutenant. Not her.

She valued his skills as much as he did hers. Neela: physics. Pier: electronics. Together: great chemistry.

The data poured through the multi-channel, multi-dimensional collectors and went directly into the computer banks. The cerampix would be studied later by scientists and the data on the block circuits run through the massive Lyman IV base computer. A dozen intricate theories on the abnormally high density of dark matter inside the Lyman system would be proven or discarded, and Norlin didn't care. It would give Neela her degree, and that pleased him. What did he care of the 'branes altering the fine structure constant?

He cared more for Neela's brain — and the rest of the package.

He ran his fingers over the control console, not watching the inexorable progression of words across the vidscreen. Trying to study for the lieutenant's examination had proven more difficult in isolation than he'd believed when he accepted this assignment. His mind kept returning to Lyman IV — and Neela Cosarrian.

Her long, blond tresses floating on the wind mesmerized him. He could watch for hours as the breeze pulled at her locks and outlined her finely boned face, that gorgeous face with bright sea-green eyes and straight nose and full lips that pressed so nicely against his.

Norlin heaved a deep sigh and ordered the computer to back up over the last ten pages of vidtext. He had seen it all but understood none of it. How could he when he wished he were on-planet with Neela?

"Status report," he ordered.

"Forty-seven analyzers are online and recording," came the ship's soft voice. Norlin frowned. He had ordered the technicians to duplicate Neela's voice. There was a slight hint of huskiness to this computer-generated tone that Neela lacked. He had been on-station only a week and already something glitched?

This oversight didn't bother him as much as the notion that they might have cut corners in preparing other equipment. He had asked for extensive modification in the bulky, bulging converted picket ship, and the spaceport techs had not received the news well after Neela, her adviser and three other physics profs had finished giving their specifications for equipment mounting.

"How many experiments running?"

"Eight. Do you wish an itemization?"

"Is Neela Cosarrian's online?"

"Yes. Doctoral Candidate Cosarrian is studying the interplay of dark matter with higher-dimensional membranes in an experiment to determine—"

"Stop," Norlin ordered. He knew the basic premise of her research. He had just wanted some contact, however slight, with her and her work. All he got was an increasingly generic computer voice.

"There is an unusual signal being detected on a little-used frequency. It is almost drowned out by the ten-centimeter hydrogen emission."

"Natural?"

"Artificial," the ship said. The voice circuit altered again and turned deeper and more male. Norlin sat up and blanked his vidscreen. On a prior flight he had noticed the subtle change in tone. The ship had warned of a fuel cell malfunction. He had repaired the trouble before it developed into full-blown danger. Since then he had become more aware of the computer's inflection and timbre.

Norlin expertly homed in on the signal, laser-bounced a request off an orbiting cometary detector forty light-seconds across the system to get a triangulation, then estimated the original frequency and corrected for the Doppler blue shift to get approach speed. A plethora of other information could have been deduced from the faint signal, but Norlin allowed the computer to follow an expert systems program rather than do it himself.

The content of the message worried him.

Through the snap and hiss of hydrogen emission, he heard the faint, worried voice warning, "Dangerous bastards. Can't use normal communications channels. They'll hear. They listen. They're clever. Destroyed my planet."

Norlin worked to computer-filter the signal further and amplify it. He made no attempt to transmit; that ran counter to his standing orders. Other research ships orbited through the Lyman system gathering data. An unexpected broadcast transmission might wreck hundreds of hours of minute signal collection. Even with sophisticated filtering, primary data might be lost by errant radio signals.

Norlin's eyes worked along the readouts on his board and saw that everything progressed well. He concentrated on enhancing the signal from the distant source. Not only did the contents tantalize him, it broke the monotony of the flight. Studying had quickly palled, and the few amusements the Empire Service allowed aboard a picket ship held his interest less than a day into the mission. He was a mere week into a three-month orbit.

Three months without Neela.

"...huge fleet. Can't guess how many. At least ten thousand, maybe more."

At this, Norlin frowned. He might be picking up an entertainment transmission from another system, though the strength of the signal belied that. The idea of ships descending to destroy a planet had been discredited by Empire strategists long years ago. The finest genetically enhanced mentalities in Emperor Arian's court had considered the problem for a decade before deciding that planetary defenses could fend off any mobile invasion. Even though such *gedanken* battles were suspect, Norlin had seen the computer results and agreed.

That didn't stop the trivid dramas from showing fourteen different worlds blowing up every week as a result of rebel invasion, alien invasion, natural causes and even unexplained phenomena. Norlin snorted. That wasn't entertainment. He preferred the real dramas from Earth's Golden Period. Nothing pleased him more than a good Sherlock Holmes drama or a well-acted Travis McGee piece, unless it was a latter-day Golden Period vid from the 2060s.

"Just my luck," he said, switching off the receiver and going back to his textbook. "Had to get some worthless trivid."

He tried to concentrate on the text on his vidscreen and found he couldn't. Something nagged at the back of his mind. He finally switched to full computer access and asked, "Is band splitting possible on any entertainment broadcast?"

"No," came the immediate answer. "All entertainment bands are laser-closed and not broadcast. What cannot be done by satellite bounce is transmitted through foptic cable. This is done for financial considerations."

He nodded. There was little leakage from a satellite bounce or a comsat origination program, insuring viewers had to pay for what they received. Through a fiberoptic cable there would be no detectible leakage.

He again worked the frequency carrying the disquieting message, wondering at its origin. While it might have been an Earther broadcast from an earlier century, the signal strength was too great for it to have come more than a hundred light years.

"Help me. Can't go on much longer. Dropped out of shift space too soon. Couldn't get back in. Too close to Lyman IV system primary for a second shift. No power, anyway. Oxygen's almost gone. Am switching to loop broadcast with everything I discovered. Don't let them destroy another world. The Death Fleet. The alien Death Fleet!"

Norlin jumped back from the console when a loud screech tore at his ears. He checked the auto-volume control and found it properly adjusted. The unknown ship had switched to a high frequency and micro-bursted several hundred terabytes of information. Norlin made sure he had intercepted it and began reforming it into usable data.

He fluctuated from complete disbelief to grudging acceptance of what he saw. The scoutship pilot had not given full documentation, but the pix of the huge black beetle-like looting factories moving along the streets and stripping away everything of value sent shivers up Norlin's spine. It might be a fake. The entertainment industry had true geniuses at duplicating reality, making their fictions seem more than real.

A graininess to the pix bothered him. He believed these photos had been taken from orbit using a scout's surveillance equipment. He was expert in sensors of all kinds. He made a guess about the model of cerampix camera used to record the destruction. Even worse, he couldn't tear his eyes from the vidscreen.

The panorama of death and devastation sickened him even as it held him captive.

"This must be a hoax. One of the others is sending me this as a joke."

He tried to locate the other research ships gathering data. He found Josi Prenn's. She wouldn't fabricate such an elaborate joke; hers tended toward sharp jabs lacking subtlety.

Two other picket ships showed up on his sensors. Both were too distant and out of position to originate the signal.

"It's broadcast," he mused. "That's hardly ever used. Signal gets too weak too fast. Better to use a lock-in lasercom." He fell silent. Lasercoms were useful when you had an exact position on both receiver and transmitter. If he believed the unknown scoutship's pilot, the man had no idea where he was or whom he reached.

Norlin ran through a complete global scan. Only the faint off-band com signal from the mysterious scout-ship broke the bubble of tenuous locator radiation he sent out. He followed it back, checking through triangulation using other detector units. The same position came out of the computer.

The distressed scoutship lay just inside the Lyman system Oort cloud. This presented too much danger for a practical joke. The area a thousand AUs from the primary was littered with small comets and particles of dust and gas trying to become comets. Norlin had heard of at least two manned probes into the area in the past year that had been severely damaged.

"Not a joke," he decided. He continued to watch what the unnamed scout pilot had recorded, the frightening view of a world being systematically ravaged. The readouts showed how the radiation cannon had scoured the planet of life before the automated wrecking crews landed.

Pier Norlin watched and thought and grew more restive. He glanced at the sensors he had locked on the probable position of the small scout craft. The instant a tiny waver came in a gravimeter reading, he jumped into action.

"Request permission to alter course," he said, flipping on his base lasercom. He started to explain then fell silent. It would be two hours before base received the request and another two for their response.

Norlin fumed at the necessary delay. He spent the next four hours on edge, waiting for the reply. When it came, he still jumped at the sharp, clear response.

"What's got into you, Norlin? You just started your sweep. There's no way I can let you off. Finish your assigned course. We can talk about durations when you get back."

He had expected it and had prepared his reasons — and tried to brace himself for more light-speed delay.

"Sorry, this is a class-three emergency. Possibly a class-two." He had run through the scout's data during the hours waiting for authorization, sending selected segments to bolster his case. The light-lag delay in approval for rescue put the scoutship in increasing jeopardy, but he had his orders. To break off the research orbit required high-level approval. Or absolute certainty on his part that he did not have. This could be a prank, although a sick one.

"Class two? There aren't any ships in distress. Don't try to feed me vacuum. Finish your mission and quit wasting my time. I go off-duty in four hours, and you've tried my patience all day long."

"Scoutship, registry most likely the Penum system." Norlin double-checked the computer's figures backtracking the scoutship. Penum seemed to carry a ninety-five-percent level of confidence as the ship's port of origin.

That meant Penum IV's colony was dead, and the entire planet raped. If this was not an overly elaborate joke at his expense.

"Here come details. I'll give it to you in a classified burst." Norlin worked for several minutes, as if his supervisor might violate the laws of physics and order him to stop immediately. "Here comes everything I got from the ship. It's going to be a macroburst. Get ready for it."

Norlin almost went crazy waiting for confirmation of receipt of the transmitted data. Four hours stretched like four centuries.

"We're getting some proton storm interference," came the unexpected reply. "Retransmit to be sure we get your data. Can't hold a beam longer than a few minutes. Stay on your predetermined course so we can maintain laser-com."

"Understood." Norlin said immediately, then cursed himself for the response that wouldn't be heard for two hours. He punched in the transmit code again. The data relayed by the scoutship in addition to his own observations blasted toward Lyman IV on a lasercom beam. Even as the computer churned out the transmission, Norlin reprogrammed his orbit to intercept the incoming scoutship. Violating orders might mean saving a pilot in extreme distress.

"Inconsistent with mission," came the computer's immediate response. "There is insufficient fuel to jet directly to intercept and finish our mission. A Hohmann orbit requires fourteen days. In either instance, the ordered data collection must be terminated."

"Rule One," Norlin said.

"Danger to the crew of a spaceship noted."

"Well?" he demanded. "Give me the mission override, and let's blast straight on an intercept and damn the fuel!"

"All pertinent data have been analyzed. There are no living crew members aboard the scoutship."

He slumped. He had hoped the pilot had survived.

"Oxygen?" he asked.

"Affirmative."

"Intercept in optimal time," he ordered. "I assume full responsibility. Even if the crew is dead, the ship contains important data."

Cold waves swept up and down his back as he stared at the vidscreen and the slow parade of black metal machines chewing their way across Penum IV's surface. The pilot had died bringing this warning to Lyman IV. What other information had he put in the scoutship?

"I require base confirmation."

"Get it," he snapped.

Norlin heard the deeper authoritative male tone in the computer now. He was in no mood to argue with a hunk of quantum-etched superconducting ceramic multidimensional nanoprocessor.

"Clearance for maximum blast obtained. Prepare for full acceleration in ten seconds."

Norlin blinked. The authorization had come back fast. That meant the first macroburst had been decrypted quickly. That anyone at the base had the sense to appreciate the gravity of the information startled him. Several new genetically enhanced officers had shipped in — personal favorites of Emperor Arian, it was rumored. All Norlin knew was that the genhanced line officers paid little attention to duty, preferring their own esoteric pursuits. Perhaps somehow, those esoteric pursuits had intersected with actual duty.

He settled into his couch just as the lateral steering jets fired. The small picket ship realigned then blasted out at full speed. The monatomic hydrogen-lox engines got the ship moving and then shut down. Then the electric ion engines applied a steady thrust that rapidly drained the fuel cell batteries. This far from the primary, Norlin could not use solar panels to replenish.

The cost and wear on the ship were not his concern. His mind raced as he tried to make sense of what he had seen. He rapid-scanned through the cerampix taken by the pilot. The dizzying array of sights and ships and destruction chewed at him.

Empire Service had found three other alien races. Two had disputed the emperor's right to colonize their worlds. Both had been interdicted and effectively confined to their own systems. It had been from these two campaigns that the emperor's strategists had decided that destroying a civilized world was impossible by fleet bombardment. The Empire Service fleet had sustained massive casualties in seven attempts on the two worlds. Even asteroid diversion had proven ineffective.

Spacefaring races operating near their home worlds had advantages a foreign invader did not. Three ES-sent world-wrecking planetesimals had been blown apart while expeditions to launch seven more had been destroyed. And look as the Empire Service might, neither of the systems had significant Oort clouds for the deflection of a comet into the worlds. Sending a snowball comet or iceteroid into an inhabited world would surely destroy it unless the target planet used efficient, effective lasers to melt the smaller, deadly incoming particles across a wide region of space.

Norlin shuddered as he thought of the third alien race discovered. The Sien had not been able to carry the war to Earth. Neither had the Empire Service been able to penetrate into the small star cluster already settled by the prolific Sien. An uneasy truce had been drawn after fourteen years of sporadic, fitful fighting. Earth observed the treaty more out of fear than honesty. The aliens had their own reasons for not venturing into further contact with the emperor's colonies.

A fourth alien race—a superior one—presented Emperor Arian with immense problems. Norlin had heard of the growing rebel bands on other worlds. He had personally seen the growing discontent of both Sutton and Lyman with the genhanced imperial line. Mutiny was becoming more common on Empire Service ships and executions for increasingly trivial offenses the norm.

Even a sub-lieutenant like Norlin saw that Earth had internal difficulties with its colonies that needed immediate attention that was not being delivered. An overwhelmingly superior alien race bent on conquest could be the element needed to break the colonies away from Earth—and possibly destroy both Earth and the far-flung colony worlds. As frightening as it was, Norlin thought that Sutton might ally itself eventually with an alien culture rather than remain a colony of the Empire.

"Where's the picture of the aliens? All I see are their robots." He grunted as he moved to give the computer more instructions. Even a half-g acceleration wore him down after a few days of free fall in space. He had neglected to do his exercises—all pilots scorned them and paid the price later when they landed.

"Scanning," the computer reported in response to his keyed orders. A few seconds later, the computer reported, "There are no photos of aliens. All moving indications are of robotic machines controlled by a master computer or a shielded intelligence. The robotics, however, are of unknown design and motive power, indicating they are of alien design."

"That's just photonic," he grumbled sarcastically. "We don't know what they look like, but we do know what their destruction does." He punched in a new string of commands. The computer responded immediately.

"Time of interception eight hours, three minutes. Recommendation: three-quarter oxygen intake to insure safe return to base."

"So ordered," he said. Always suspicious of automated life support equipment, Norlin checked to be sure the computer had adjusted the levels properly. He felt a little lightheaded, but he was trained to operate at even lower oxygen levels. What held his attention came from a sensor panel, not life support.

"What's giving the indication? We're still too far from the scoutship for visual." He tapped in a quick command in an attempt to isolate the briefest of flickers on his readouts.

"Vidscreen image enhanced to max," the computer reported.

"I don't see any—"

Norlin bit back his denial. He didn't see anything, but something moved through space an AU away. Space black, it moved without showing jets or ion trail. The only way he knew it was there was by the occultation of a star pattern he knew well.

"Estimate size of object," he ordered.

"There is no object within sensor range," responded the computer.

Norlin's heart skipped a beat. At this distance, with sensitive research-caliber sensors, the ship could track a rocky nugget the size of his skull. But the computer had not detected anything where he had seen the stars wink out.

There was only one explanation. The aliens had arrived in the system — *his* star system.

Chapter Three

N orlin worked to keep the scoutship centered in the vidscreen. His external visuals were limited; most sensors relayed information in the infrared or the far ultraviolet. Other research ships carried astronomical gear in the visible spectrum.

"How far?" he asked the computer.

"Another day's travel. The scoutship is at the limit of vidscreen range."

Norlin snorted. The computer didn't tell him anything he didn't already know. He worked on the image and magnified it to the limits of the equipment. The graininess increased to the point of turning the smooth contours of the scoutship into bumps. Infrared was not optimal for the information he desired most, but he had to work with what the ship had been outfitted with.

He backed off and studied the hull. From this distance, he saw no trace of damage, as would have been evidenced by hot spots.

"What about the alien vessel? Report status of detection."

"Lasercom report to base is being maintained."

"What's the lag time?" Norlin patrolled the outer fringe of the system now. The time delay had risen to eight hours while he had been accelerating; the delay time to reach base and get a response amounted to sixteen hours. His sense of isolation and danger mounted with every passing instant. The sight of the minuscule scoutship, apparently undamaged but turned into a spacefaring coffin, bothered him greatly, as much for the apparent death aboard as the information the pilot had taken with him.

His attention turned to another sensor. The black ship sliding all but tracelessly into the Lyman IV system gave him a sense of foreboding, because he knew it had been there, even if his ship's sensors had failed to locate it. Norlin was not inclined to hallucinations and didn't doubt for a microsecond that the ship had been from the alien Death Fleet in the scout's report.

"They're coming. Did they follow him? Or have they done their own scouting work?"

He kept his far-flung sensory bubble of feeble radiation at its limit. He jerked when a chime sounded, alerting him to another contact.

"Full detail. Turn everything we've got on the alien ship," he ordered.

"This is pointless and counter to instructions," complained the computer. "Many experiments will be ruined if all sensors are used."

"Do it." Norlin's finger hovered by the override button in case the computer balked. It didn't. He heard gears grinding as mechanical mounts shifted to sight on the alien ship.

He had no idea what types of radiation the other ship might emit. IR? UV? His densitometers and gravimeters had been designed for use on molecules subtly interacting with dark matter, not spaceships. He pushed them all to the limits of their design. Let the scientists complain later. A grim smile came to his lips. This might cost

Neela her degree, but he would make it up to her. If this ship—or ships—was the vanguard of the Death Fleet, continuing experiments would be pointless. Survival would be the only important pursuit.

He hesitated, almost reran the pix of Penum's rape. Only iron will prevented it. The images played over and over too clearly inside his skull—possibly etched there forever.

"The ship is smaller than a cruiser," came the computer's analysis. "There are no outward indications of armament. A few robotic appendages for unknown operations dot the hull. Other than these, there is nothing hostile about the craft."

"What radiation emission?"

"Negligible. Interior shielding for transuranic pile is excellent. Power leakage is minimal."

"Don't you find that suspicious?"

"It is efficient."

Norlin cursed. The computer struck to the heart of the matter. Except for its surreptitious entry into the system, the ship had committed no hostile act. It was only his imagination and the evidence from the scoutship that condemned the vessel as an aggressor.

He almost tried to lasercom the stealthy ship. It might be from another race, a fifth intelligent spacefaring alien culture, fearful of meeting humanity straight on. From the alien viewpoint, this might be business as usual. Norlin's fingers danced over the computer console. The odds against finding two new alien races in such a short time were astronomical—this ship belonged to the same fleet that had devastated Penum.

Nothing else made sense.

He magnified the alien ship's outline as much as possible to see the external grapplers mentioned by the computer. At this range, he failed to find them other than by faint heat signatures. Norlin leaned back and worried his lower lip as he thought. This wasn't a warship. What was its purpose? Grapplers for manipulation of cargo? That served no purpose. What might the ship find that needed repair that the crew need not handle?

"Scan and find," he ordered. "Item: scoutship report. Initial entry into Penum system of unknown spacecraft."

He watched with increasing anxiety as the pilot's report began to match with what he was observing. He returned to scanning the alien vessel. No, it wasn't a peaceful scout from a race wary of contact with humanity. This ship had crept into the Lyman system and sought out the cometary detectors as it had in the Penum system. The small craft sneaked up and used those robotic appendages to reprogram the detectors to ignore the Death Fleet when it entered their range. They had done this before, according to the dead pilot of the scoutship. They were doing it again. Now.

The aliens took no chances. Their assault came without warning because of careful preparation.

Norlin entered his observations and sent them on the lasercom to base. Let the emperor's genhanced tacticians work on the data.

If the aliens risked exposure slinking in to reprogram the detectors that meant they could be defeated in all-out battle. They minimized their danger of finding a world ready to defend itself. Norlin shuddered. They had reduced genocide to an efficient program of entry, alteration of sensors, full-scale invasion and destruction and complete looting.

He finished his report and dropped off in an uneasy sleep, trying to keep both the alien craft and the scoutship on the split-view vidscreen. When he awakened, his neck muscles had knotted and his shoulders throbbed.

The scoutship hung only a few thousand kilometers away. The computer had guided an approach, decelerated and matched relative velocities in far less time than expected.

"Full scan," he ordered.

"Performed," came the computer's answer. "Do you wish to enter? It is dangerous and not recommended."

"I'll do it anyway. We need all the data we can on the aliens."

"Base has confirmed your speculation on the alien's operating plan. You are to return directly to base with minimum delay."

"How long?" Norlin asked. He slipped into the transfer skin hanging by the airlock. The thin nanocloth clung to him with electric tenacity. He smoothed the wrinkles, slung the backpack containing the oxy-helium breathing mixture and slipped the airhose into its connector before dropping the helmet onto his shoulders. The momentary tingle that assured him an airtight seal had formed faded. Around his waist he fastened a toolbelt.

"With maximum acceleration," the computer responded, "eight days."

"Eight? But—"

"You will sustain an acceleration of two-point-three gravities."

"Fuel?"

"Sufficient," said the computer. "Hurry in your current mission. We must launch in forty-seven minutes."

"Don't leave without me," Norlin said almost flippantly.

He experienced an odd euphoria as he cycled through the airlock, sighted on the distant scoutship and triggered his backpack's chemical jet. With constant thrust, he reached the ship in less than ten minutes. All the while, he thought about the alien advance craft and how it must be locating and modifying the deep-space detectors.

He touched down easily on the scoutship's hull and shuffled toward the airlock. He frowned when he saw fabric in the locking mechanism. That told a grim tale of death he did not want to consider at the moment.

He cycled open the hatch. No familiar gush of air met him — the lock had been vacated and never refilled. He pulled the cloth free and saw by the name patch that it belonged to an Empire Service maintenance tech named Benks. He tucked it into a pouch once he got inside the airlock. He had more worries than how this had fouled the locking mechanism.

Inside the cramped ship, he checked the atmosphere. The carbon dioxide levels were dangerously high, and the oxygen too low to sustain life. The pilot lay sprawled across the control console, a notebook clutched in his hand.

Norlin quickly examined the small cockpit and tucked the cerampix and the computer memory blocks into his pack. As he worked, an automatic camera recorded everything in detail.

"Poor bastard," he muttered when he finally examined the pilot. On impulse, he turned off his recorders before prying the notebook free from the man's death grip.

Norlin read silently of how there had been four, then two, who shifted for Lyman IV. The pilot had been afraid of his passenger, especially after the man had cold-bloodedly murdered two coworkers. Norlin's heart went out to the pilot, who had known his own life hung suspended on a slender cord.

The last page in the notebook detailed how the pilot had murdered the maintenance man Benks and shoved him through the airlock in shift space.

He straightened, sticking the notebook into his belt. He turned on his recorders again and established a comlink with his own ship.

"Time, please," he requested.

"Launch window opens in fourteen minutes. It will remain open for seven. The gravity augmentation from planet V will no longer be available after this, adding a full day to travel and placing fuel use at an unacceptably high level."

"I'm returning. Prepare for launch but do not initiate the final sequence without my direct command."

"Understood."

Norlin wondered if there was anything more he could do for the pilot. The man lay across his console, killed in the commission of his duty. Norlin couldn't think of a more fitting memorial. He saluted and cycled back through the airlock. For a moment, he paused, then bled out the gas inside the ship. The pilot would remain in this crypt for eternity, never decaying, always at his post.

As a final gesture, Norlin took the notebook from his belt and flung it away from the ship as hard as he could. He doubted the ship's puny gravitational attraction would pull it back—or that anyone would ever find this silent tomb again for it to matter if it did.

But to Pier Norlin it did matter. Let his report of the pilot being a hero go unchallenged. The admission of murder never need be mentioned.

He jetted back to his ship and prepared for a week of double-gravity hell.

※ ※ ※

"I don't understand," Norlin said. "Please repeat."

He frowned as he scanned the orbital docking station above Lyman IV. His was the only ship locked into the spiral. The emptiness of a once-busy station coupled with the odd orders worried him.

He checked under his seat for his Empire Service-issue pistol. The magazine popped out easily, and he saw the neat lines of ETPE-propelled caseless rockets inside. He rammed the magazine back into the pistol butt and thrust the weapon into his belt. This was far from regs, but he had no time to find the holster and strap it on.

"Leave your ship and report immediately to Captain Emuna." The blaring command from his console speaker made him jump.

"I want to report directly to Commander Clarkson."

"Sub-Lieutenant Norlin, do as you are ordered."

"I don't know Captain Emuna. What division is he assigned to?" He almost repeated his question because of the time it took to receive his answer.

"He was deputy supply officer."

Norlin shook his head. A supply officer? Emuna didn't even rank in the table of organization. He was little more than a nuts and bolts counter, a bureaucrat and not a line officer.

Norlin powered down the ship, leaving it on standby. As tiny as it was, he thought of it as his own—his first command. Deep down, he knew that he might never see it again.

"Goodbye," he said softly. Then he checked the pistol stuck in his belt, made sure a rocket had been properly chambered and the safety thrown. He left without a backward glance and wiggled into the spiral.

The corkscrew design provided easy docking for more than fifty small picket ships. He went "down" the zero-g spiral toward the main station, every sense straining for a clue about what had happened. This area was usually filled with workers and pilots, coming and going and just loitering. He saw no one. Even the robot workers had been deactivated.

The situation turned even grimmer when he entered the main station. On a slow day there might be five hundred men and women working in the dispatch center. It was eerily empty now. A few computer vidscreens winked and flashed, but their operators were gone. Even the quiet whir of the electrostatic precipitators constantly cleaning the air of all dust particles had fallen mute. The station had been put on standby condition, just as he had left his ship.

Tense, hand on his pistol, Norlin walked slowly along the echoing, curved corridors. The only sounds he heard were ones normally hidden by the bustle of activity. Air circulated sluggishly. Lights emitted a high-voltage hum. His boot soles, with their magnetic strips, clicked as he carefully measured each step.

The farther from the center of the station he went the more the spin tugged at him and created pseudo-gravity. After a full week at more than twice normal G, he felt strong, quick, able to contend with any problem.

He stopped in front of Commander Clarkson's office. When he saw the laser burns on the steel door, he drew his pistol. He checked cautiously and found the office empty. Someone had staged a vicious battle inside, though. Holes were blasted through the walls using weapons similar to the one he clutched in his hand. Energy weapons had reduced portions of the bulkhead and decking to molten puddles that had recrystallized. Norlin found no trace of his commander and his staff— or their fate.

He stopped by a console that had been knocked from an under-officer's desk. A few seconds' tinkering brought up a display he could use.

"Query," he said. "Identify. Captain Emuna."

The voice response required adjustment; he barely understood it. He switched to full vidtext and scanned the information. He let out a lungful of air he hadn't even known he was holding.

Emuna was an army supply officer and nothing more. For command to have come to him all senior staff—and most of the junior officers, as well—had to be gone. From the carnage in Clarkson's office, Norlin guessed that "gone" meant "dead."

"Details of mutiny, please," he requested.

The rapid flood of text revealed the worst. There had not been one mutiny but four, each more violent than the preceding one.

"Every two days for the past week," came a tired voice from the doorway behind him.

Norlin spun, pistol ready.

"There's no need," the man said. His shoulders were slumped, and the dark circles under his eyes showed sleep had eluded him for some time. His uniform hung in wrinkled folds, and his hands shook uncontrollably.

"Captain Emuna?"

"When you didn't report directly to my office, I knew you'd come here. Not a pretty sight, is it. You should have seen it when Clarkson made his first stand."

"He survived the first mutiny?"

"The second, too. He and the genhanced officers the emperor sent. They were the ones the staff objected to. What they did to them when the third attack was successful is something you'll have to find in the files. I can't bear the thought."

He swallowed hard, his scrawny neck showing a prominently bobbing Adam's apple. Emuna wiped sweat from his upper lip and sank into the only intact chair.

"You're the ranking officer?"

"Out of almost a hundred, I'm it. There are a few lieutenants running around—all were in my division. Ironic, isn't it? The noncombatant unit on-station survived. I don't know space dust about running things. I order, I deliver, I make sure everyone has toilet paper and fattening food and porno cerampix. And here I am, station commander. Want some hot porn?"

Norlin pushed the safety on and thrust the pistol back into his belt. Captain Emuna presented no threat. He could spit on the man and knock him over. The strain of command showed in every line indelibly etched on Emuna's gaunt face.

"You received my report?"

"That's one reason all this happened." Emuna gestured at the ruined office. "Emperor Arian has been less and less popular out here, you know."

"But...mutiny?"

"Why not? Who wants to defend a world under the emperor's thumb? Better to shift out and find a rebel world where you can be free and away from all the madness passed along by the genhanced geniuses he sends."

"Some *are* geniuses," Norlin said.

"Most are deranged — and that is being polite. *Unstable* is the word I hear most. But they're all space crazy. Dangerously so. Who wants to die for them?"

"You saw the report. The alien Death Fleet will wipe out all human life in the system when they arrive. I discovered a scoutship tampering with the cometary detectors."

"We found out about that almost immediately. They disable the sensors then put in a repeater giving bogus information so they can sneak in past our warning nets. When that information leaked out, it triggered the last mutiny. Anything that could space was hijacked. I swear some men put out in packing crates. Clarkson had already died, him and the genhanced Earthers. I forget who tried to stop that uprising."

"The vice-commander was…?"

"He died the first day. Someone used a pistol like the one you've got on him. Right through the head." Emuna tapped his temple. "Blew his brains all over a bulkhead. We sealed up the room rather than clean it."

"You realize that I'm ranking officer," Norlin said. "I'm in the line of command, since I'm a pilot."

"It's yours. No arguments. Take it. The whole damned station is yours to do with as you please."

Norlin stood and stared, open-mouthed. He had expected argument. He received only full cooperation.

"I don't know what's going on. I try to keep things working. Most of the station is shut down or on standby, not that it matters. There are fewer than a hundred left to man it."

"A hundred? But the full complement is eight thousand!"

Emuna shrugged. "They left. They died. They're no longer around for one reason or another. And you're in charge. What're your orders, Commander?"

Chapter Four

Pier Norlin started to speak then clamped his mouth shut. Everything Captain Emuna had just said looped infinitely through his mind. A supply captain—an army supply officer, at that—could never be in the chain of command for a station, much less a space command base. Hearing the man so easily pass over command, and to a sub-lieutenant, shook him, though.

"I...I know you're right," Norlin said carefully. "You've been running the station for how long now?"

"Almost forty-eight hours. That's the last time I slept, at any rate." Emuna yawned and stretched. "I was never psychologically stable enough for field command. I try to do everything myself. No capability of delegating authority. What are your orders, Commandant?"

Again Norlin hid his shock. A sub-lieutenant outranked no officer except ensign. For him to take command of a major Empire Service facility, he had to be called by something other than his true rank.

Commandant Norlin. He liked the sound of it—and it frightened him. He had neither the experience nor the ability to command the immense station. Training as a pilot had hardly prepared him for this. The notion of preparing the station to defend the entire system frightened him even more. He, of all people, knew intimately what they faced, and how difficult the battle would be.

He stared hard at Emuna. The man had become a psychological mess in just two days. He could do better. He was a space pilot. He had the training and the ambition. The promotion had just come at a time when no one was likely to appreciate whatever he accomplished.

"What were Commander Clarkson's standing orders?" he asked.

"Can't say—his vault was completely destroyed. It wouldn't do much good getting in, anyway. We'd need the code to decipher the memory block once we got it into a reader. I tried to contact sector base on Sutton Two, but I had to send a message packet. There weren't any couriers available."

"An automated packet?" Norlin gulped. That was the least reliable method of reporting—important messages were sent by courier ship. The drone missile with the message might not arrive precisely on target, it might be ignored for days or even weeks—or it might vanish during shift. Fully twenty percent of the robot probes never shifted free at the end of their flight.

Maintaining the delicate balance in a shift engine required constant attention—attention a human gave far better than any AI system because during shift electronics went subtly wrong.

"What ships are in dock? I can refit my research ship and shift out. I'll need to drop in an engine module after discarding most of the research equipment. It'll be cramped but enough supplies can be squeezed in."

Norlin dreaded the idea of shifting almost forty light-years to Sutton II by himself. The trip would take almost a month. He had been alone too much lately.

A new thought filled him with dread.

"Wait. What about conditions on-planet?"

"Can't say. The last report I saw carried a time stamp of five days ago. With the station in mutiny, the ground bases lost control. Two were in the hands of rebels — or mutineers."

"Widespread civil unrest?" Norlin thought of Neela Cosarrian at the university.

"You know someone down there? Better see if you can't arrange to have them lifted to orbit. Reports are sketchy, but it doesn't look good — and it's been five days."

Norlin considered the matter. He was in command now. The idea still shocked him that he could do anything he wanted, within reason. A slow smile crossed his face. It didn't even have to be reasonable. Commander Clarkson had issued orders often that bordered on the illogical.

He stiffened and pulled his shoulders back. He could do better. He *would* do better. He was an officer in the Empire Service.

"Send a ferry down to the university. I want several students and faculty brought to the station immediately."

Emuna shook his head sadly. "There's nothing to send. Your picket ship could land. Maybe take off again, though I can't say."

"It's equipped for planetary landing," Norlin said.

"You're the only pilot left on the station. The rest are dead or gone. Where do you think all the ships went?"

"The pilots all mutinied?"

"The only reason the hundred crew are left is inability to find a way off the station. Who wants to be at ground zero when your Death Fleet arrives?"

"It's not my Death Fleet," Norlin said defensively.

"You reported it. You're the only one who has seen any of the ships." Captain Emuna wiped the sweat from his upper lip again, his eyes taking on a frightened-animal aspect. "You probably beat them here by a day, at most. We don't have long to live. They're going to kill us all, just

41

as they did on Penum." The officer's voice rose shrilly. "I saw the pix. I know what they did. Radiation beam us to death then strip the entire damned world."

Norlin edged toward the door, uncomfortable facing the growing madness in his fellow officer. He backed outside the office then went exploring in an attempt to find anyone else who might be in charge. The few pitiful souls he found were all civilian support staff and were more frightened than Emuna.

He went to his quarters and punched in his access code. The interior hadn't been looted like many of the rooms. He snorted contemptuously. He had nothing worth stealing, even if the mob had broken in.

Settling in front of his console, he began his inspection of the station.

The conditions were worse than anticipated. Within a couple days all life support systems would fail due to lack of maintenance. He passed on getting the robot workers back to their duties and tried to contact other humans to help. He failed. Those he reached wanted nothing to do with him. Without the infrastructure of a military base to back his orders, he was powerless. Even if they acknowledged his command position, and only a handful of the hundred survivors did, they were both fearful and contemptuous of any Empire Service officer.

Norlin didn't blame them. The Empire Service had brought on this crisis. Ignoring the ones left in power might not restore order, but it prevented further dissolution.

"Attention, all personnel," he announced after cutting into the public address system. "This is Commandant Norlin. Report to the officers mess, ring fourteen, sector nine, within the hour for a briefing."

The handful he had not spoken to directly might come to see if they could get off the station. Enlisting their aid might be impossible, but he would know who he had to cope with.

He checked his pistol and immediately went to the mess. He had thought it would be a suitable spot for his briefing. Now, he wasn't sure. A fire fight had melted most of a major bulkhead. He climbed through the slagged wall and crouched on the far side. It gave scant protection against heavy armament but ought to keep him safe from hand weapons.

Norlin ducked when he heard the whisper of cloth against metal. Someone slid along the corridor wall outside, trying not to be seen.

"Drop the weapon," Norlin ordered as he thrust his pistol through the hole in the wall.

The smallish man he frightened spun and brought up a pistol.

The training Norlin had received in data analysis sent him through a chain of reasoning that almost cost him his life. The pistol was a fully automatic version of his, with a clip carrying twice the rockets. He saw the gunman: beady eyes squinting hard, mouth pulled into a thin line, finger turning white as it pulled back on the trigger. He estimated time and distance and intent. He should have fired before the other man.

A stream of self-propelled rockets blasted from the pistol and blew through the bulkhead all around him. His response came from surprise rather than thought or training. Norlin's finger jerked back.

The single rocket he fired caught the gunman in mid-chest and blew white bone and red blood all over the corridor.

"Why'd you do that?" he asked aloud, bewildered. His gorge started to rise when he saw the body.

Then he forgot the man entirely — four others pushed through the door on the far side of the mess, all armed.

This time he did not think; he reacted. Eight rockets finished the first three men. By the time his comrades lay blown apart on the deck, the remaining mutineer had his laserifle up and firing. The continuous beam hummed and sputtered. Molten steel spattered Norlin's back.

He dived forward, skidded and got off three more shots. One rocket blew apart the bulkhead beside the rifleman. This distracted the man long enough for Norlin to get in a killing shot.

He picked himself up off the floor and walked on shaky legs to the view the carnage he had caused. He stared at the exploded bodies, as if looking at a distant, barely recognized trivid picture. Then he vomited.

When he recovered, he picked up the last man's laserifle and slung it over his shoulder. He felt the need for more firepower. If Captain Emuna's estimate was right, he had just killed off four percent of all those remaining on the station.

Neela. I've got to get to her. It must be even worse on-planet.

He wandered in shock, his mind refusing to focus properly. He rounded a corner and stopped, jerking out his pistol and aiming it at a bulky woman sitting on a low table, her short, stocky legs crossed and her colorless eyes fixed on him with a hot intensity that made his skin crawl.

"Don't shoot me, hero. I'm not armed." She held out her hands, palms up. He saw grease and calluses. This startled him enough to burn away the shock. No one got their hands dirty with robots and telepresence remotes everywhere, and she looked as if this was a regular condition.

"Who are you?" he asked.

She wore shapeless regulation overalls, but he thought he saw tarnished lieutenant's bars under the grime on her collars.

"You the pilot of the picket ship? The one who made contact with the Empire Service spy boat?"

"Yes." Norlin shook himself. He was in command of the station, not her. He'd ask the questions. "Who are you? You never answered. You look like a repair tech."

"Not even close. Ship's Engineer Barse." She hopped down. Her square-cut dark hair and curiously pale eyes were below his line of sight by a full twenty centimeters. She shoved out her hand. He shook it, almost gasping at the power in her grip.

"I watched as you docked without the magnetic grapples. You did a good job. Real smart piloting."

"Thanks," he said. "I do what I have to."

"You ever been on anything bigger?" Her colorless eyes fixed on his rank and stayed there. She seemed to be evaluating him and wasn't liking everything she saw.

"I've never piloted anything larger," he said, "but at the academy I copiloted a hunter-killer."

"Those pieces of space debris?" Barse spat a thick gob of brownish scum that stuck to a wall and sluggishly flowed to the deck. "Not fit for man nor genhanced beast."

"They're fast and deadly. Kilo for kilo, there's nothing with more armament. They are certainly better than an unarmed research ship," he said.

"But not better than a cruiser."

"Nothing's better than a cruiser, except a battleship."

"Not even those hunks of slow armor," Barse asserted. "They're easy targets. Can't shift as fast. Big profiles. Heat signature that makes me puke. Leak radiation up and down the spectrum. Any genius bomb can take them out. Too easy to spot. Not a cruiser. Not one like the *Preceptor*. It's state of the art." She puffed out her considerable chest in pride. "And I helped refit her."

"I've never heard of the *Preceptor*," Norlin said. "Is it a new arrival? I'd heard rumors that a couple new ships were due in."

"It's been in dry dock for months. Top secret. Captain Dukker's private toy. Or it was."

"Dukker? Isn't he one of Emperor Arian's...?"

"One of the emperor's toadies? He was. Son of a bitch got his head blown off in the first mutiny. For a genhanced genius..." Barse openly sneered when she spoke of him. "...he was one damned fool. Walked right into the middle of a mob, demanding that they disperse. They tried to rip him apart, but he was too strong, so they blew his head off. Even then he fought on for almost a minute. Goes to show he never used that genhanced brain of his for much."

"Who's in command now?" Norlin asked.

Emuna had said no one in the chain of command was left, but if the cruiser's outfitting had been classified he wouldn't have heard a whisper. The copilot could assume command of the station, being a space officer.

"No one. That's our problem."

"You've not got a copilot? Was he killed, too?"

"Dukker was a one pathetic son of a bitch," Barse said, "but I'll give him this. He could pilot his way through a black hole if he had to. Never liked the notion of someone sitting at his elbow. No copilot. Just crew."

"Crew?"

"Miza, Sarov and Liottey, in order of their smarts."

"Where do you rank?" Norlin asked, a slight smile curling his lips.

"At..." Barse stopped and stared at him. Her expression altered subtly, and her pale eyes took on a glitter like amethyst. "You're all right, Norlin. We're going to get on just fine."

"What are you talking about? I'm in command of the station, and you're assigned to a cruiser."

"You're in command of space junk." Barse spat again. "Is there anything worth saving here? You just turned the guts of five men into novae. Think there are any better left?"

"You scanned the information on the Death Fleet. We've got to prepare a defense for Lyman IV. The station has heavy artillery. I don't know how much and I can't remember when it was used last—certainly not since I've been here."

"Never is my guess. There's rust on the lasing tubes." Barse spoke with such authority that Norlin hesitated to argue. Lasing tubes weren't likely candidates for rusting. Most were formed from carbon composite materials, and the chambers were highly silvered. The chemical shells that fitted into the firing compartments might have deteriorated, but he doubted this. Storage in the hard vacuum of space had definite advantages.

"There are civilians on-planet. Our oath of duty is to protect citizens of the Empire."

"Piss on the Empire."

Barse watched as he lifted the pistol. He aimed it unwaveringly at her chest.

"That's treason," he said. "We are both officers in the Empire Service and have duty and honor to uphold."

"Piss on the Empire," Barse repeated, "but you're right. I did swear to keep its stupid civilians from getting blown into decaying atoms. You've got a choice to make."

"What choice is that?" Norlin asked. He lowered his pistol but did not put on the safety. Barse wasn't hostile enough to be a mutineer—he hoped.

"You can stay with this outmoded, outgunned hunk of junk and die in a futile attempt to stop a fleet of space knows how many warships." She pointed at the station around them. "Or you can come aboard the *Preceptor*. We've got a full complement of crew—except for a pilot."

"Me? Pilot a cruiser?"

"I was outvoted. The other three want a human on the bridge. I know a computer can do it all and better. It'd take a bit of tinkering, but I could kludge one together in a few days."

"We may not have a few days. There may be only hours before the alien fleet comes in, radiation cannon firing."

"Dammit, I know. That's why I decided to go along with them. You want to pilot a top-of-the-line cruiser or not? It's going to be your last chance."

"Command a cruiser? I'm better qualified for that than garrison duty." Norlin's heart skipped a beat. Piloting an Empire Service line vessel was the goal of every officer.

"No one said anything about command. You'd be under my command."

Norlin looked at her then laughed out loud. He tried to stop and couldn't. Tears ran down his cheeks, and he clutched his sides.

"That's the funniest thing I ever heard. An engineer can't command."

"Calm down. You're hysterical," she said, accurately assessing the true source of his mirth. "That's the way it's got to be aboard the *Preceptor*."

"What do the others say about that?"

"They agree."

"Then you'll have to look for another pilot."

"You'd stay on this derelict and let the Death Fleet blow you into undifferentiated protoplasmic plasma?" Barse's eyebrows arched in disbelief.

"We'd all be dead in seconds if I agreed and tried to let you command the ship. What do you really know? I may not have much experience, but I've been trained."

"I'm the best damned engineer in the Empire Service—and I outrank you."

"You probably are the best engineer," Norlin said. "That's not got a damned thing to do with commanding a ship's crew, though. You're right about a computer being able to operate better. A good pilot lets the computer do what it does best. A commander knows how to keep humans and machines working together smoothly. There's more to keeping a ship running than being able to navigate."

"Damned little else."

Norlin heard the vacillation entering Barse's voice. She knew he was right and was reluctant to admit it. He turned the argument against her, proving his point as he did so.

"Decisions. They have to be made by reaction, not conscious thought. An AI system computer can come close, but there's always the unknown. They're programmed to randomness if they're unable to make a choice given current data. Who do you trust? A machine's choice of random data or a human's? Mine?"

"So, you admit you might make the wrong decision," she challenged.

"Maybe, but the odds are still with a disciplined pilot. I'd try to keep my own hide intact. An AI system doesn't have that programmed into it. What keeps me alive just might keep you alive — and the cruiser in one piece."

Norlin remembered the long, arduous training he had endured. Most of what he did at the console came as second nature. A cruiser would be a challenge, but he was better qualified to accept it than an engineer or computer operator.

"We got fed up with Dukker pushing us around."

"He might have been a good pilot, but he sounds like a lousy commander."

"You ever been in command?"

"Not before an hour ago." Norlin smiled crookedly as he stared down the station's long corridor. "It's been a challenge, but it's time to move on. I'd like the chance to be the *Preceptor*'s pilot — and commanding officer."

"Damn," muttered Barse. She wrung her hands then stared up into his purple eyes as if she scanned his soul. Norlin could almost see the decision process she went through.

"Call me Tia," she said finally. "We run an informal ship."

"Call me Captain Norlin. I don't."

Chapter Five

The *Preceptor* is standing off the station a few klicks. We didn't want to get involved in all this."

Tia Barse wrinkled her pug nose as she surveyed the main docking area's destruction. Norlin had missed this demolition by coming in down the picket ship corkscrew. The major ships docked here had presented major opportunities for escape; dozens of vessels had been hijacked by mutineers.

"Do you have a shuttle or did you use a bubble suit?"

"I held my breath and walked. I'm tough."

"You're an engineer," he said, shrugging it off.

Norlin wanted to see his new command and discover the problems he would have with the other three crew members. Barse had made it clear she'd accept his orders if they seemed reasonable—and possibly not even then. That bothered him. In the heat of combat, and having access to full computer information, he might try a tactic that seemed suicidal. If the engineer balked the others might, also. He had to establish who was the *Preceptor*'s captain early.

"You've got style, kid."

"That's *Captain* Kidd, to you, Lieutenant Barse."

"Got it," she said insincerely. "There's the two-man shuttle I used. Want to jet across now?"

Norlin's mind raced. He had new responsibility in the cruiser, but it hardly seemed right to abandon his command on the station without putting someone in charge. Such desertion in the face of an emergency constituted a court-martial offense. That no one of rank remained to charge him—or would ever know—didn't deter him.

"I've got to find Captain Emuna and turn command of the station back to him."

"He's not in the chain of command. He's nothing but a toilet paper counter. I ran into him a couple times. What a pain in the butt he was. Double forms this, triplicate that and where's your captain's aunt's grandmother's DNA-confirmed authorization?"

"I don't want to walk away without letting him know I've relinquished command."

"You take all this seriously, don't you." Barse cocked her head and stared at him, those unblinking colorless eyes boring into his soul.

"Would you want it any other way?"

"Not on my ship," she agreed.

Norlin found a console that required only a few minutes' tinkering to get working.

"Captain Emuna to any com."

He waited only a few seconds before the officer's haggard, haunted face appeared.

"You're leaving? I'm on the bridge and saw the cruiser come up."

"You've got the conn, Captain. I'm going to the *Preceptor* and assume command. It's the best way of fighting the Death Fleet."

"It doesn't matter. I tried checking the number of staff left." Emuna heaved a deep sigh. "There're only a few aboard the station. We can't put up a decent defense—*any* defense. We're goners."

"Captain," Norlin said sharply. "We are Empire Service officers."

"You are. I wasn't anything more than an accountant."

"Not a very good one, either," Barse muttered.

"Captain!"

The other man reached for a pistol. He put it to his head and broke the circuit. Norlin heard nothing, but he imagined the sound of the weapon firing and the explosion within the captain's head.

"Rough way to go," commented Barse. "If he'd thought on it for a second, he could have gone down fighting the alien fleet. Would have amounted to the same thing."

"We'll see," Norlin said, his belly tied in knots. He had graduated from the Empire Service Academy with more idealism than he'd thought. Pragmatism had been drilled into each cadet, but Norlin had believed the officer corps to be more loyal and responsible than he'd seen.

Mutiny. Suicide. If any remained, would they attempt to collaborate with the aliens? He pushed the horrible notion from his mind. He hoped that any human would die fighting rather than turn traitor to his own race. No one, nothing organic, had been left on Penum. The aliens had sent their pillaging machines to get things; humans would only have been in the way.

"Let's go," he said. "I'll conduct a brief inspection, then I need to go down."

"On-planet?" Barse peered at a vidscreen showing Lyman IV hanging suspended in the jet-black sky. Thin wisps of snowy clouds formed into force ten storms over the primary ocean—falsely named Tranquility Ocean by overzealous promoters and developers looking for colonists in the early days.

The four major land masses stretched brown and gray and green and brought a lump to Norlin's throat. It looked so much like Sutton II.

He had been born on Earth but remembered little of it except the pollution, overcrowding and rank-conscious

53

populace. He had thought of Sutton as his home after arriving there for academy training. It looked so much like Lyman he hated to think of it laid to ruin, too.

"There are several people I need to find."

"Why bother? They're ground grippers. Otherwise, they'd've been on the station when the mutinies started."

"*Civil unrest* is the way Captain Emuna described conditions on-planet. Have you anything more to add to his report?"

"No, Captain."

Norlin's eyes widened in surprise.

"Is there anyone you or the others want to contact on-planet or try to lift off?"

"No one for me. This isn't my world — or my type of world. Can't say about Miza or Sarov. And I don't much care if Liottey has anyone there. He's a vacuum brain."

Norlin interpreted the woman's evaluation of the others in the *Preceptor*'s crew. She didn't care for Liottey. He couldn't tell if it was personal or professional dislike. The other two Barse had a guarded truce with.

He followed her into the small shuttle and wiggled forward to lie beside her.

"Ready, Cap'n?" Barse didn't wait for his answer. She slammed home the locking lever and pressurized the bullet-shaped shuttle in the same movement she launched them toward the cruiser.

Norlin took the acceleration on the bottoms of his feet. He felt lightheaded for a few seconds then recovered swiftly. Barse had intentionally launched fast to test him. His week at more than two gravities stood him in good stead. He reached over and put his hand on hers atop the throttle.

"Cut back. I'm in no hurry. I want to study the station's exterior."

"We can take a quick tour by the defense turrets," she offered. He nodded assent. She worked the throttles expertly and fired side jets to turn the shuttle. The off-vector thrust caused a roll.

Norlin never hesitated. He pushed her away and took over. The tiny ship righted itself.

Barse silently allowed him to conduct his survey of the immensely powerful chemical laser turrets studded all over the space station hull. Norlin's heart sank when he saw that the engineer might be right about rusty lasing tubes. The exterior showed no sign of maintenance for months, possibly years. Micrometeorite pits pocked what should have been sleek surfaces.

The rebel attacks had been directed at worlds other than Lyman IV, allowing the garrison to become lax. Even if a full crew remained to man the laser cannon and kinetic projectile weapons systems, they'd have a difficult time making their equipment function properly.

"Enough," he said. "Take us to the *Preceptor*."

He turned the controls back to her and settled down on the thinly padded couch, lost in thought. Defending Lyman would be more difficult than he had thought—and his first impression had been one of desperation.

Barse docked the shuttle in the cruiser's huge cargo bay. Norlin barely noticed the details. He had seen cruisers before, and the *Preceptor* looked no different from standard designs he had studied at the academy.

His mind ranged out and down to the planet. Neela Cosarrian needed him.

He swallowed hard. It went beyond that. He needed *her*. He missed her soft touches, the feathery kisses that turned into true passion, the shared moments afterward. All that would vanish forever if he didn't get her off the planet before the Death Fleet arrived.

"You all right?" asked the engineer. "You're shaking."

"I've got to go down right now," he said. "Is there a ferry?"

"We can refuel your picket ship. We might have to rip out everything in the equipment bay. That any trouble?"

"No. It's modular."

"You don't need the electric ion engine, either. Reduce weight, increase fuel for the rocket."

"See to it," he said. "I'll conduct a quick inspection of the *Preceptor* and then be on my way."

"You got it, Cap'n. Give the boys and girls my best." Tia Barse wiggled around and let him out. She resealed and jetted off even as he opened the inner airlock and saw the interior of his command.

His. Shock at such a major promotion under war conditions struck him anew.

"You're the sub-lieutenant Tia found on picket duty."

A small, dark woman stood with arms crossed, glaring at him. Her head had been shaved on the sides, leaving only a thick scalplock of jet black. Woven into the topknot were silvery strands and what looked like sensors.

"I use them to augment," she explained. "I plug them into the computer and get a dozen new inputs. Some are light prompts, some aural and a few turn warm or cold."

"You're the computer op."

"How astute, but then, Barse said you were fast." Cold eyes darker than space raked him. She rocked back slightly in obvious distaste for one so young commanding her cruiser. "Chikako Miza, Sub-commander with nine years of space duty."

"Pier Norlin, Captain, recently graduated from Empire Service Academy on Sutton II."

"Captain?" Miza said cynically. "They're turning them out young. You must know people in high places on Earth."

"I know how to pilot, I know how to command. I assume you know how to run your department as efficiently."

He spun and faced a man his own height but twice his girth and bulk. Like the computer op, the man stood with bulging arms folded in an aggressive manner. He had bristly dark hair cropped down almost to the point of being shaven off. Thick, bony brow ridges hid muddy brown eyes. A feathery network of scars crisscrossed his left cheek.

"Sarov? Engineer Barse has spoken well of you." Norlin turned and glanced back over his shoulder. "Of you, too, Miza."

"What about me?" came a soft, almost feminine voice.

Norlin frowned when he saw Liottey. Whereas Barse looked manly, the first officer had a distinct effeminate appearance. Sandy hair piled in unruly curls toppled from his head into a knot tied on the side. Blue eyes Norlin could describe only as beautiful peered at him from behind long lashes. Liottey saluted. Long fingers ended with decorated nails.

"Report on our condition, Lieutenant Liottey. Critical status systems only."

He felt odd ordering about men and women who were not only superior in rank but also in age and experience. Liottey was easily five years older, Miza ten and of the stolid Sarov he could make no guess. The bulky weapons officer might be ten or even twenty years older.

"Engineer Barse has everything shipshape, Captain," Liottey reported. "We need only do the final vectoring checks, and we're ready to whip our weight in aliens."

"We'll have to do better than that," Norlin said drily. "We're a single ship against an entire fleet that numbers in the thousands." He turned to Chikako Miza. "Contact Barse and determine how long it will be until I can drop down to the planet. After that, we can start a shakedown cruise."

The woman tipped her head to one side and touched a silver bud in her scalplock. "She pulled the equipment and the electric ion drive. There wasn't any authorization to get for refueling—or anyone to honor it, even if she had bothered. Your ship is ready. Barse will have it in the cargo bay in ten minutes."

"So fast?" Norlin realized then how capable his engineer was. Even with a full complement of robots working at her orders, the stripping and fueling had been done in extraordinary time.

"She likes engines better than people," sniffed Liottey.

"I would, too, if you were the only human aboard." Miza mimicked the man's tone then said, "I'll return to my duty station, Captain, unless you need me for something important."

This time, the sarcasm stung like acid.

"Dismissed." Norlin needed to maintain some hint of authority. The crew calling him by his title helped, but their tone showed no deference. He had yet to prove himself. They might not know it, but he did—they could all be cooked by the aliens' radiation weapon before they acknowledged him properly.

"Do you want me to accompany you?" asked Liottey, as eager as a puppy. He had already begun to wear on Norlin's nerves.

Loud enough for all three to hear, Norlin asked, "I'm going on a rescue mission. Do any of you have relatives or friends you'd like retrieved?"

"You'd risk your neck for my friends?" asked Miza. Her cynicism dropped for a moment then rose again like a palpable mist. "There's no one on this rock worth the effort." She stalked off, returning to her computers.

Mitri Sarov shook his head once.

"No one. We just arrived from Earth," said Liottey. "I haven't had time to make many...friends."

"Very well. Prepare for the shakedown run when I return."

"Should you go?" asked Sarov. "Barse had trouble finding us a pilot—any pilot. To risk your life is to risk our mission."

"I'll be careful. Thanks for your solicitude."

Norlin pushed past and went back to the cargo bay airlock and waited for Barse to dock. She pulled the smaller ship in close enough for him to run a flexible 'lock extender over and magnetically grapple it to the steel airlock ring. He hurried back to his first command.

Cramped as it was, the research ship had become his home. He felt comfortable inside. He knew its quirks—and its simplicity of operation.

"All yours, Cap'n," Barse said. "How do you like the crew?"

"I just hope Liottey doesn't get to liking me too much," he said, grinning crookedly.

"If he does, just let me know. I'll put him in his place. I eat executive officers for breakfast."

"Don't. He might clog the engines if you stuffed him too far into the venturis."

Barse laughed and slapped him on the back so hard his teeth rattled.

"You're going to be just fine. If you can pilot, the *Preceptor* is going to be the hottest ship in space."

Norlin held back his retort—it might be the *only* Empire Service ship in the entire Lyman system.

He waited for Barse to uncouple and pull back the extensible airlock then hit the jets. He shot away from the cruiser's bay, oriented himself and calculated his descent. Fuel was of little concern—Barse had filled it to the hull after removing the equipment and ion engines. The ship was light and more responsive than he had ever experienced.

He plunged downward, correcting constantly, using unconscionable amounts of fuel as he visually located the university and circled above. He was not challenged, and the planetary nav system wasn't operational.

From an altitude of two kilometers, the campus appeared calm. Using his sensors and magnifying the pix showed a different world. Buildings had windows knocked out. The computing center had been razed, and smoke still spiraled upward from the ruins. Huge craters had been blown in grassy areas once populated by students, and several of the research laboratories he was familiar with had been turned into burned-out husks.

His heart almost stopped when he thought of Neela caught in the middle of such mob action.

Norlin fought the buffeting as he hit denser atmosphere and brought his ship down near the lab where Neela had an office. He winced as his exhaust cut through one wall and spectacularly brought down a nearby administration building. The structure exploded with a ferocity usually reserved for fulminating barrage shells.

The true destruction, though, had preceded his landing. He killed the jets and left the ship on standby.

"You will not launch unless I use emergency code sequence *Neela*," he ordered. He didn't want anyone tampering with his ship or trying to hijack it while he sought his girlfriend.

"Understood," the computer answered. He noted the huskiness and the baritone timbre that betrayed immense stress.

Norlin adjusted his belt comlink to the cruiser, checked the weapon tucked in his belt then unslung the laserifle. The readout showed almost full energy. He had at least a dozen shots at full power and three times that at half-power.

He left it on maximum and exited the ship.

Acrid smoke bit into his nostrils. On all sides were the sights and sounds of devastation. The rioting had happened days ago, he judged, but the smoldering fires and slow deterioration lingered.

Hurrying toward Neela's lab, he saw a few people duck from sight like cockroaches in sudden light. He decided they were too far away to do him any harm, and getting into his ship would be impossible using anything less than a monatomic hydrogen cutting torch. He worried more about what they had done rather than what they might do. He clutched the laserifle a little tighter as he trotted toward the lab.

"Captain?" Liottey's voice, over his comlink. "We're picking up incoming vessels. Miza thinks it's the leading element of the Death Fleet."

"Acknowledged," Norlin said, touching a stud at his belt buckle. "I'll hurry."

"Miza estimates an arrival time within the hour. Those fellows are coming in fast—and none of the cometary detectors let out a peep. They're following the same pattern as on Penum. So far."

Norlin didn't respond. He pushed past the debris blocking the front entrance to the astrophysics laboratory and stared up and down the length of the marble-floored corridor. He felt as if he had walked into an elevator shaft—and there wasn't an elevator there. His stomach fell endlessly and his breath came in quick, harsh pants.

Much of the lab equipment had been thrown into the corridor and smashed. He ran toward the fifth room on the left—Neela Cosarrian's.

"Neela!" he called, not expecting to find her.

Her computer console had been ripped out, and its tough PLZT ceramic screen cracked. He used the muzzle of the laserifle to push through the debris, hoping for some clue to the woman's whereabouts. The search would take forever.

"Liottey!" he barked into his comlink. "Can you locate individuals on-planet?"

"There's a chance Chikako might be able to tie into the master computer at Empire Central Control" came the answer. "I'll check."

Static almost drowned out the words. Norlin frowned. The reception had been good before. The breakup in communication might be the result of alien action. Neutralize contact, swoop in, kill, rape, pillage and retreat. Repeat in the next star system.

"Who do you want?" came Chikako Miza's peeved voice. Norlin told her. Miza snorted, then broke off for several seconds, coming back with "Got it. She's in the police computer as a dissident wanted on a variety of charges."

"Not Neela!"

"She started a riot the first day after news of your discovery leaked. Hmm, she was involved, at least. Hard to tell if she started it. She certainly knew those who did."

Norlin nodded. Neela's politics *were* more radical than his, and she knew many campus activists; but she would never be part of wrecking her own lab. Her research meant more to her than anything else. Norlin swallowed hard. Her membrane-dark matter interaction project would have been a career-maker. She might well have valued it far more than she did him.

"Where is she?"

"They have her jugged in a temporary lockup in the building next to the one you're in. At least, they had her there three days ago. That's the last entry anyone bothered to make."

Norlin raced from the lab and burst into the sunlight. Except for the more visible destruction, he found it hard to believe this world was in any turmoil. Wind whistled softly through the trees in the green areas. The blue sky had enough fluffy white clouds to hide the sun every few minutes and put to rout the rising summer heat. The humidity made it pleasant.

Then he caught a whiff of smoke.

Burned meat. Burned human flesh. He managed to keep from gagging as he raced on.

He was so intent on reaching the next building he didn't hear the whistle above his head. When the second rocket launched, he saw the flare and dived onto his belly. The rocket swerved and tried to home on him. It blasted a small crater in the ground a few meters behind him.

Norlin swept his laserifle in a circle and turned the side of the building into slag. He didn't wait to see if he had killed the sniper. He got to his feet and ran on, smashing into the wall, spinning and plunging into the interior.

He fired at a moving object. A woman let out a scream and fell backward, pistol falling from her lifeless hand. Norlin kicked the weapon away and began a systematic search for Neela. He gagged when he saw the corpses in the first three makeshift cells. Someone had penned the victims inside and blown them apart with a rocket pistol.

The men in the next two cells were little better than dead. They stirred feebly. Norlin tried to interrogate one.

"Neela Cosarrian. Where is she?"

The man reached out weakly. Norlin opened the cell door and hurried on. He had no hope that the man might capitalize on his freedom, but it was all he could do for him.

He found her in the last cell. Norlin wouldn't have recognized her except for the blouse she wore. He had given it to her on her birthday two months ago.

"Neela!"

"Pier? They put me in here. Dr. Scotto tried to rescue me..." Her voice petered out. She collapsed in his arms. Norlin swung her over his shoulders and lifted. She hadn't been fed in days; she was feather-light.

He reached sunlight again and stopped. Two men, armed with rocket pistols prowled around the ship. These weapons lacked the power to breach the ship's lock, but they were more than adequate to blow him and Neela into atoms.

Thoughts of honor and duty and his oath to protect the civilian population flashed through his head. Pier Norlin lifted the laserifle and touched the trigger. A deadly bolt of coherent radiation erupted and turned one prowler's head to vapor. The other returned fire.

By this time, Norlin had started across the grassy lawn separating him and Neela from escape in the ship. The man fired wildly; the rockets never came close enough to lock onto them.

A second bolt from the laserifle sent the man scurrying for the cover of a burned-out floater car. Norlin kept firing and forced the man to stay down. The laserifle left little more than sludge where the car had been; the man sought safety farther away.

Norlin tossed away the rifle when it sputtered, its magazine exhausted.

"I put the energy to good use," he said to Neela. "I got you back."

He gave the 'lock opening sequence to the ship and heaved the woman inside.

"Close, prepare for lift-off," he ordered.

The ship did not respond. He cursed. The two men must have somehow damaged the computer.

"A tank leak has been detected. Fuel is critical," the computer said. "Is the added cargo necessary?"

"Cargo?" Norlin cried, outraged. "You're talking about a human."

No response. Norlin turned to where he had laid Neela on the floor. Her eyes were closed, and a look of serenity had erased the pain that had been there when he first found her.

"It'll be all right," he said, cradling her head in his lap.

"There is only one human aboard," the computer said. Again came a long silence. "She is no longer alive."

Norlin panicked. He pressed his fingertip against Neela's throat, searching for a pulse. He found none. His hand under her nostrils detected no exhalation. Prying open one of her eyes, he saw only a fixed pupil. There wasn't any reaction to light.

"No!" he cried. "You can't die on me! No!"

"She is dead," the computer repeated. "Fuel is critical. Please unload any unnecessary mass."

Pier Norlin held back the tears as he dragged his lover outside and laid her near the exhaust tubes. He couldn't give her a proper burial. Cremation would have to do.

"Launch," he said in a choked voice. "Get us to the *Preceptor* as quickly as fuel allows. Launch code Neela."

The computer said nothing. Lights dimmed as power shifted to the control circuits, and the engines ignited. Norlin was crushed into his couch. Only then did he cry. The tears streamed back across his cheeks and spattered on the bulkhead behind his couch.

It was all he could do for her, and it wasn't enough.

Chapter Six

Sloppy work, Cap'n. You knocked the hell out of the docking tube." Tia Barse glared at the damage he had caused by his inattention to the wash from the side jets.

"Close the bay doors. Either jettison the research ship or secure it. I don't care what you do. I'll be on the bridge."

"Hold up, Cap'n," called Barse. "What happened down there? Didn't you find your friend?"

He turned a bleak expression in her direction. She read the full answer before he said laconically, "I left her."

Norlin couldn't bring himself to say any more. The idea of Neela vanishing in the exhaust tore at him as much as the memory of the widespread destruction on-planet. The population hadn't waited for the Death Fleet to kill them. They had started rioting and done much of the aliens' work.

As he stalked through the *Preceptor*'s shoulder-wide corridors, he conducted a cursory inspection. Each compartment he glanced into seemed neat, clean and everything he could want in readiness. He might not have acquired a good first impression of Gowan Liottey but the XO had done a fine job of keeping the vessel shipshape in the absence of a captain.

By the time Norlin arrived in the control room, he had his emotions hidden, if not under complete control. The ache remained deep inside; he doubted it would ever go away.

"Report on the Death Fleet's position," he snapped.

Chikako Miza ran her fingers through her hair, lightly brushing and stroking the silver ornaments there as if she played some musical instrument. Seconds later, a trivid picture coalesced around her head, giving Norlin the sense that she was at the center of the universe and he, an outsider, peered into her world.

Tilting her head to one side, she got a distant expression in her ebony eyes, as if she listened to the ancients' music of the spheres. Only then did she reply.

"They're braking hard. I've picked up Cherenkov radiation from the trailing ships of the fleet. Only a few of them were an AU inside the system. The remainder were in shift and are homing in on the leading elements."

"Numbers?"

Norlin slid into the captain's swivel chair. His hands shook as he settled the heads-up visor on his head so it covered his eyes but left downward vision clear. By turning in different directions, he saw every instrument aboard the *Preceptor*. By shifting his eyes, he isolated the data he needed. A simple touch to the brim of the HUD visor locked in a particular display. Norlin had no interest in most of the readouts. He settled for a summary display from each station.

"Locked onto three thousand war ships," said Miza. "They're going to burn us out of here."

"How many following them?"

"Twice that," she said. "I'm counting in one, two, many mode. There are more of them on the way, and they know who's been naughty and nice. It's not going to be a good Christmas for us."

"There can't be that many," Norlin snapped angrily.

"How many does it take to blow us out of space?"

He ignored her jibe and shook his head, trying to clear his vision. "How do I get rid of some of the summary displays? I want ranging, I want nav, not what I've got."

"Punch it into the arm of your chair. I'll redo," Miza said.

Norlin glanced down at the arm of the command chair and saw the small keypad. His fingers seemed too large and clumsy for such precision instrumentation, but he found the right sequence to obtain the information he wanted regularly. The HUD still glowed with torrents of data, but he was trained to assimilate and act at this rate. Or so he thought.

For a split second, he thought he'd gone blind. The bright flash of the display reprogramming faded and left only the terse summation of readouts he wanted.

"What happened?"

Miza said, "All planetary sensors are gone—burned out by alien EMP. Let me cut those feeds from your circuit."

"Thanks." He set to work making certain the *Preceptor* was ready for combat.

Norlin fell easily into the role of ship's captain. This was exactly like his training in academy simulators, but after a few minutes he began to feel the pressure of command, of making the right decisions.

"Waiting for authorization to arm," came Mitri Sarov's calm baritone.

Norlin swung around as the summary display changed to the tactical officer's setup. He nodded. Sarov knew his job. The *Preceptor* wouldn't vanish from space without one hell of a fight.

Sarov had expertly arrayed their missiles; neither he nor Norlin saw any reason to power up the heavy lasartillery. The greater the distance at which they engaged the

Death Fleet, the better off they were. If they came into laser cannon range, they wouldn't last ten seconds.

"Begin launch at your discretion," Norlin commanded. He watched as the first flight of missiles blasted free. Vibration coursed through the ship as new missiles auto-loaded into the electromagnetic rail launchers. Flight after flight of the heavy projectiles left the cruiser's tubes, hurling outward without betraying jet flash. Only when the missiles were light-seconds away did the rockets kick in and the internal homing devices begin hunting for suitable targets.

"Monitoring flight path." Sarov lounged back, locking his fingers behind his head. His work was done for the moment. The ships in the Death Fleet would find themselves under attack from all directions — and with no obvious attacker in sight.

"Computer analysis of chance of success," Norlin requested.

Sarov bent forward and pressed a single button. The result flashed on Norlin's HUD, but the tac officer still gave his verbal report.

"Deceleration and the resulting radiation emission blocks their detectors. Our sneak circuits are good; the missiles are almost undetectable. Projection is ninety-five percent contact."

"Destruction rate?"

Even as he asked, Norlin knew it was impossible to estimate. They had no idea of the alien ships' quality of armor, survivability or control systems. The missiles carried warheads varying in type from solid projectiles with kinetic activation to small power drills that bored into hull metal and then exploded. Even if the enemy couldn't detect them, they might be able to take incredible damage and still fight.

"Launch a dozen atomics," Norlin said.

"They might detect the transuranics. Also, those warheads launch slower than the others."

"Put them on independent mode and launch."

"But—"

Norlin gave the bulky tac officer no chance to argue. Of Miza, he asked, "Is everything clear?"

"Your course is laid in."

"Liottey?"

"What is it, Captain?"

"Report, dammit! Life support? Incidentals secured? Give me everything."

"All aye, Captain. Sorry."

Norlin snorted. He glanced in Liottey's direction and scanned the XO's summary displays. Life support appeared nominal. He didn't have time to double-check the rest of the officer's responsibilities.

"Engineering, give me full control."

"The engines are begging to be abused," Tia Barse said. "Whip 'em till they bleed. Then they'll ask for more."

Norlin craned his neck and picked up the summary display from the engineering station located aft of the main bridge. As with the other summaries in his HUD, all looked good.

"Liottey, join Barse in aft engineering. If anything happens, you're in command. Understand?"

"But, Captain Norlin!"

Norlin wondered if Liottey refused to obey because the bridge lay in the center of heavy armor, vibration dampeners and reactive shock defenses while where Barse toiled was just forward of her precious engines and vulnerable to an ass-end missile shot. Although he had never heard of a situation where the bridge had been blown off and the remainder of the ship survived, he wanted there to be some small chance of the *Preceptor* limping away if he died.

"Do it. Now!"

He turned back, not caring if Liottey obeyed or not because things had heated up fast. His proximity display flared red with danger. The Death Fleet was almost on top of them.

"Blast—now!" He sagged into the chair's pneumatic cushions as the mighty engines sent them hurling along their orbit around Lyman IV. He kept a full navigational display parading in front of him. Using the planet's gravity well to slingshot the *Preceptor* away, he gained another advantage. For a brief time, he used the bulk of the planet to shield the ship from the Death Fleet.

"There goes the station," came Sarov's deep voice. "They hit it with atomics. Six, eight, twelve bombs of fifty megatons each. Good shell temperature on detonation. Upward of ten eV. Nice design on their devices."

Norlin changed the view in his HUD from readouts to external. In vivid three-dimensional display, he saw the expanding cloud of superheated plasma that had been the system's most heavily fortified base. With full defensive armament in action, the station might have held off the alien attack for hours. He checked and found no outlier residual ionization cloud to indicate anyone had attempted to interdict the deadly alien missiles.

"Goodbye, Captain Emuna," he said softly. The officer's body was now nothing more than scattered ions. "It wasn't a choice post for a first command."

"First missiles finding targets in their formation," advised Sarov.

"Effectiveness?"

"Good. I'm reading sixty-seven percent destruction rate. We can kill them."

Norlin jerked around, more from instinct than instrumentation warning. He worked frantically on his computer console, wishing he could speed up input by using voice control. Even though the computer differentiated voices, no captain allowed voice during combat. If the hull was breached, they might lose atmosphere. Such a pressure change altered the frequency of a voice and often resulted in computer rejection.

Norlin also suspected that too many combat officers developed a dry mouth and found it difficult to enunciate clearly enough for the computer's acceptance. His own mouth tasted like desert sand.

"Cap'n," came Barse's voice over an isolated command circuit. "How're we doing?"

"A scoutship spotted us leaving orbit. It's after us. Miza will pick it up in a few seconds."

"You got it before her? That's rich. She owes me a liter of whiskey. She claimed you'd — "

"Engineer, what do you want? I'm busy."

"Sorry, Cap'n. If your mouth's going dry, Dukker always kept a small tube of thirst-kill in the left arm of the chair."

Barse clicked off, and Miza's cold tones informing him of the scout's detection replaced the engineer's more pleasant voice in his ear.

"Already working on it," he informed her. She mumbled to herself when she saw the computer had already begun feeding Sarov fire control coordinates.

"Want the lasartillery brought up to full capacity? We can take a ship of that mass. We outpower it."

Norlin toggled his acknowledgment of the request and denied Sarov's desire to engage. Full power remained on the drive engines. He launched a small missile and watched the scout easily deflect it.

"We're in for a battle," he said over the general circuit.

"Let me — " Sarov started.

"Quiet, Lieutenant-Commander. Run AI battle plan projections, mark seven, mark nine, mark ten."

"Very well...Captain."

Norlin let Sarov work on the preprogrammed combat control programs to see if any of the three offered a good chance for survival while he studied the alien scout with growing uneasiness. It massed a tenth of the *Preceptor*'s bulk, but it moved well, and something about its aggressive pursuit showed that its crew had no fear of them.

He had seen how they surreptitiously reprogrammed sensitive cometary detectors to allow their entire fleet to enter a system unchallenged. The aliens' knowledge of human technology had to be good; those aboard the scout knew they faced a fully armored cruiser.

"They've turned their radiation cannon on us," came Miza's and Sarov's simultaneous warning. The displays went crazy in Norlin's HUD. He ripped off the command visor and turned to the slower readout on his control panel.

"Damage?"

"Engines are still running. I've got them on manual, though. That bastard took out all my auto-control circuitry," reported Barse.

"Sir," came Liottey's wavering voice. "Life support is damaged."

"Then fix it, dammit." Norlin punched off Liottey's individual circuit. The only way Liottey could reach him was through the general circuit they all shared. He doubted this would keep the XO from whining, but ridicule by the others might hold him in check for a while. By then, the *Preceptor* would either be safe or an expanding, superheated ball of high-Z plasma.

"Combat control, what are the best weapons for on-the-run fighting?"

"Missiles. We can lay them behind us like a mine field and make it more difficult to follow."

"Lay them along our course and set them for random detonation. Have a few lay doggo and then lock on after the scout passes them. Get him from behind. Keep the intruder vessel busy!"

"No indication any other alien craft is onto us," came Miza's cool appraisal. "It wouldn't surprise me if they thought the scoutship alone could take us."

"It might be able to," said Norlin. He turned his attention to the main body of the fleet. Even though he had a hundred different command decisions to make, he couldn't take his eyes off the vidscreen.

The Death Fleet moved into orbit around Lyman IV with eerie precision. Each ship fit perfectly into a matrix of destruction. Rainbow-colored beams licked at the planet's surface. Norlin increased magnification and saw the resulting devastation.

Buildings remained; people, plants and animals died instantly from the ionizing radiation. In a few spots, the Death Fleet dropped a deadly curtain of neutron bombs that blanketed the landscape. The explosions flared in silence and forced the computer to adjust for violent intensity changes. The blast damage on-planet remained small; only life was lost.

"Getting some reports on their fleet, Captain." Sarov's voice cut through his growing despair. "Our missiles destroyed nine of their craft. Fourteen more were damaged. They remain functional, however. Six missiles have struck the scout craft pursuing us—all inflicted less than detectible damage. That's one tough mother."

"Keep tracking."

Norlin studied the damage within the *Preceptor* and decided they had weathered their first battle in good condition. Barse and Liottey had robot repair units—RRUs—hard at work to fix the worst of the damage. No structural or major-systems damage had been inflicted.

The brief brush with the scoutship's radiation weapon had played havoc with their controls, however. Entire banks of superconducting ceramic block circuits had to be replaced. Replacing or reprogramming would take precious time. And from what Norlin could tell, the brunt of the radiation had left their engines at half-capacity. A smile crept to his lips. Barse would be fit to be tied at the alien impudence, damaging her engines.

Norlin saw how the scout avoided their missiles; the aliens had learned his tactics from the destruction meted out to their main fleet and had already relayed this to the pursuing ship.

"Request permission to recharge lasartillery, Captain. We diverted power during the fracas."

"Denied. We need the juice to keep moving, since we're limping along at half speed. The scout's overtaking us."

"We can't get any more delta-vee out of the engines, Cap'n," came Barse's voice. "Control is still spotty. That radiation cannon of theirs is one hell of a nasty weapon."

"Sarov, can we fight? What are our chances?"

"The computer's giving us less than a ten-percent chance. I don't believe this. It's only a scoutship!"

Norlin chewed his lower lip. They had little chance of fighting the smaller vessel and living to brag about it. Outrunning it held little promise, either. Without consciously wanting to, he shifted so that he stared into the vidscreen display focused on Lyman IV.

The Death Fleet had finished scouring the surface of all life. The gravid mother ships disgorged ferries and the automated factories that stripped the surface. Within days, everything of material worth would be removed from the planet, and they would go unmolested on their way to another human colony.

Norlin swallowed hard. He had already lost what mattered most on the planet. Neela's body floated as vapor in the atmosphere.

"We run. Give it all she'll take, Barse."

The *Preceptor* shuddered as the scoutship began a serious attack that caused warnings to flash across his control panel. Even fleeing as fast as they could, the cruiser sustained increasing damage.

They couldn't fight; they couldn't run.
All that remained was for them to die.

Chapter Seven

He's on us like epoxy," Chikako Miza reported. "No matter what maneuver you try, he's there and countering us. He knows what you try before you do it."

"His weapons are coming up," said Sarov. "He'll be at full power in a few more seconds. We don't dare take another full hit from his radiation cannon."

"Add another layer of shielding to the bridge," ordered Norlin.

His neck had developed knots in muscles he hadn't been aware of possessing. The constant flood of information across his HUD kept him constantly on alert trying to get the best picture of their trouble. He wanted to take a few minutes off—to catch his breath, to have a nice, long, cool drink of the former captain's amino-acid-laced thirst-kill and then return to the fray.

The alien vessel wasn't likely to pull back enough to give him any respite.

"Permission to power up the lasartillery," asked Sarov.

"No, we need the energy for the engines. We either stand and fight or run like hell." Norlin bit his lower lip hard when he said that. He was the *Preceptor*'s captain.

He had no need to explain his orders. The others only had to obey and know he had good reasons for the command. Norlin realized how new he was at this—and how unlikely he would be to gain more experience.

"What are the computer projections on the AI systems maneuvers?" he asked Sarov.

"None stand a chance. I tried several other likely candidates, based on the general schemes in each of the plans you suggested," he added, as if to assuage Norlin's hurt pride.

Norlin was more interested in finding a way free of the alien scoutship with its impossibly potent arms and dense armor. He could lick his wounds later. First, he had to fight through to *reach* "later."

He tapped the keyboard on his chair arm and saw that none of the usual evasion paths looked as if they would provide escape.

"More force shielding added, Cap'n," came Barse's voice in his left ear. "I had Liottey power it up. He needs something to keep him busy. He's so scared he's cratering."

"I'll see to it." Norlin reactivated Liottey's direct circuit. To his first officer, he said, "I need maximum shielding. Keep it up. The scout is going to hit us with the radiation cannon again. Keep me apprised of the danger levels."

He clicked off before the obsequious XO could answer. This served a small purpose and kept the man busy while the others tended to their duties.

Norlin blinked up a more complete summary display on the life support systems, since he doubted Liottey would be paying as close enough attention to them.

"Pre-discharge corona observed," reported Sarov. "We're in for another shot."

The tactical officer had barely warned them when Norlin cringed. Warning lights flared across his board and in his eyes from the heads-up display. He worked quickly to assign damage control to Liottey and Barse. The engineer didn't need to be told what to do. Liottey was increasingly harried and unable to make good decisions. Norlin cut him out of the command circuit. He could issue orders and push console buttons all he wanted; they would do nothing without first going through Norlin's display for approval. That added to his personal burden, but any mistakes the XO made in life support might kill them all.

Just as any mistake Norlin made could. What should he do? What? What?

"Was it necessary to put him in trainee mode?" asked Barse. The engineer had noticed instantly what Norlin had done.

"Yes. We've got big problems. Are you close to returning full power to the engines?"

"Right, Cap'n. Count on us. Some of us."

"Radiation damage to controls minimal this time," Miza warned. "We're in for a bigger dose, though. The enemy's powering up again. Rapid cycle time. That's one hell of a cannon."

Norlin precessed the *Preceptor* then applied thrust at a vector that almost wrenched him from his chair. The ship responded well. It had been made for abuse—and the heat of battle. The violent maneuver helped them avoid the sweeping beam of the radiation cannon.

"We've got to fight. We can't run," said Sarov. "That's a computer decision as well as mine, Captain."

Norlin nodded, although neither his tac officer nor the computer could see. His fingers tapped rapidly to spray out a thin shield of missiles, each with a different intercept and detonation characteristic. He hoped one might lie doggo long enough for the scout to pass it. A shot directly up the alien's tailpipe would finish it.

Norlin sagged when one missile after another exploded prematurely, detonated by the flashing radiation cannon. The alien's detection system proved too good; they had been alerted to know what to look for by the survivors in the Death Fleet. Another way to destroy the scout had to be found.

"Are you on the nav, Captain?" demanded Miza. "We're three light-seconds from Lyman. The Nereid Cluster of asteroids is ahead."

"I know," Norlin lied.

An idea came to him. They couldn't outdrive or out-fight the scout. They might dodge through the small cluster of asteroids that trailed Lyman IV at a libration point. He checked for size. Two asteroids were a half kilometer in length. The rest were too small for the use he intended.

Norlin twisted the *Preceptor* around violently again. Liottey complained. No one else noticed — they were too intent on their computer readouts. Sarov was the first to understand what Norlin intended.

"Power up on the lasartillery now, Captain?"

"Do it. Power down for maneuvering," he ordered her. "Get ready to give it all we can on offensive weaponry."

His HUD went black when the scout hit them squarely with a blast from the radiation cannon. The computer struggled to cut in backup displays. Norlin ended up with only minimal control over the ship and even less in the way of direct information about its condition. Not one system in ten appeared on his HUD.

"Get me nav data on largest asteroid only," he ordered.

Miza furnished him the data he needed. Norlin sent the *Preceptor* twisting in a crazy spiral and then turned the ship end for end and applied thrust. The cruiser did not come to a complete stop relative to the asteroid; it didn't have to.

"Fire at will," he ordered Sarov.

As the tactical officer laid out his program for destruction, Norlin added a few touches of his own using two missile tubes. The lights dimmed when their full battery of lasartillery fired. Norlin felt the auto-loader shaking the vessel as it slipped more missiles into magnetic launch tubes.

He blinked when his summary display returned unexpectedly. The first thing he did was check the scout's progress.

"Good shooting, Mitri," he said.

A continuous-wave laser had sliced off a portion of the scout's aft. Both missiles had penetrated the alien's effective defensive system and blown away another chunk of hull. Spectrometer readings showed a tremendous out-flux of gas; they had breached the hull and spilled atmosphere.

"Keep after him. Blow away everything that might be a weapon. Try to save the bridge module, but don't try too hard," Norlin said.

For the first time since the scout locked onto them, he leaned back and took off his command visor. The control room seemed less alive, less vital, less real without the heads-up display superimposed on his field of vision. Norlin swiped at the sweat on his forehead, stood and stretched, then dropped back.

He was captain. He still had work to do. Lots of work.

"Damage report," he requested of Liottey.

"Working on it, Captain. Are we going to be all right? I tried to follow the battle. Is the alien dead?"

"Working on it, Lieutenant. I want full systems back in ten." He toggled to Barse's circuit before Liottey could reply. "Engineering. How are we doing?"

"High load sent a Dirac function spike that wrecked a few circuits. No major problems I can't deal with, though. Just don't want more than ten percent power for the next hour or so."

"Will we blow up if I ask for eleven percent?" Norlin wasn't sure if he was joking.

"Trust me, Cap'n."

Displays winked back on in increasing numbers. He checked the repair progress. RRUs worked diligently on the worst of the damage and clever computer work on

Miza's part promised the *Preceptor* would not be entirely helpless if another alien ship spotted them. Norlin saw that he had, by and large, a good crew.

"Detectors at max. I want to know if another alien is coming after us."

"No distress signal from their scout was detected. He died without a will, Captain." Sarov scanned every possible frequency and combination of frequencies the alien might have used. Norlin breathed a sigh of relief. It would be a few minutes before the aliens noticed the loss of a scout unit — or maybe longer.

"Launch a retrieval unit. I want anything that's only slightly bolted down brought back for study. Stow the booty in the cargo bay."

"That's dangerous," spoke up Barse. "We might be bringing in a mine or time-delay bomb."

"Do it. Have Liottey see to it." Norlin grew weary of finding work for the first officer to do. He understood fully why Barse and the other two hadn't wanted to promote their executive officer up to captain, even if he *had* been a pilot.

"External retrieval unit on its way. This is the best ERU in the Empire Service fleet," bragged Barse. "I designed it myself."

"Have it work faster," cut in Miza. "We're getting company. This time it looks as if they sent the big boys. Two cruisers, if I read their transmissions right."

Norlin swore. He settled down in his command chair, settled the HUD and slowly scanned the full 360 degrees in the control room. Each instrument popped up in the wavering display. Most he noted and ignored. Some he had no idea what they meant; he ignored them, too. The ones showing how much fight the *Preceptor* had left demanded his full attention.

He knew they had been lucky. The asteroid had given them the chance to lie in wait for the scout. They had taken it by surprise with the full force of their weapons. Two cruisers outgunned and out-powered them. He had to hope they couldn't outrun him.

Even as the thought crossed his mind, a plan formed—a desperate one, but possibly the *Preceptor*'s only hope.

"Get the ERU back."

"It's just begun slicing away at their weapons module," protested Barse. "We can strip that baby naked!"

"Get the ERU back or leave it. We're shifting out of here."

"No!" Four voices chorused as one. Chikako Miza's cut through the protest.

"Norlin, you'll murder us all. No one can shift this close to significant mass. That asteroid's almost solid iron. Everything will blow up—us included."

"What is the shift field radius?" he asked.

"Fifty klicks, maybe more. There's no good way to judge since the engines are out of synch," came Barse's appraisal.

"Get us a hundred away from the Nereid asteroid. Then we're shifting for Sutton II. We've got too much valuable information to lose."

"You'll kill us."

He couldn't tell who repeated that, but to his surprise Mitri Sarov came to his defense.

"It *is* desperate, but it serves two purposes. The asteroid will explode from the shift wave radiating away from the generator. My computer analysis shows it will destroy both cruisers."

For the tac officer, that settled the matter. Anything that destroyed more of the enemy was a good plan, even if proved suicidal.

Norlin checked and saw that Barse had docked the external retrieval unit. It had laser-cut off a complete weapons turret from the scout. He hoped it had left enough of the radiation cannon intact for study. The scientists on Sutton II needed something tangible to work on. The cerampix of the battle might prove interesting, but an artifact always delighted engineers.

"Everybody button up. We're taking a flyer," he said. From all quarters, he got warnings. Drive warnings that they were too close to a large, material body. Weapons computer warnings that the cruisers had sighted them and had radiation cannon pre-discharge coronas building. Life support systems warnings of impending oxygenation failure.

Norlin ignored them all.

"Distance one hundred kilometers. We're gone!" He engaged the nav computer and hit the manual override for engaging the star-spanning shift engine.

The explosion at his back ripped his command chair from the deck and sent him spinning through the control room. Pier Norlin's last impression was of the forward control console growing large at an incredible rate. He struck with bone-breaking force, and the universe went black.

Chapter Eight

He couldn't decide where the pain came from. Each time he moved, knives stabbed his chest. The effort of lifting even one eyelid drove photonic needles into his brain. Worst of all was the knowledge that he had failed.

Pier Castor Norlin, commanding his first real ship, had failed. He had been killed in action and had lost the lives of his crew.

New pain came to him. Someone shouted in his ear.

"He's alive. The automedic is scanning him. We'll have a hologram of his innards in a few minutes."

"I hope he's still alive. I want to kill him with my bare hands. He ruined my goddamn engines!"

"There it is. The automedic shows nothing serious. He took a good whack to the skull."

"Is that the scientific term for a trauma?"

Norlin forced open both eyes and stared up into a bright light. The automedic worked quietly at his side, cool metal probes pressed into his bare flesh studying his organs for damage. A green light blinked, giving him a clean bill of health.

"You've got cracked ribs. The 'medic's medicating you for that now," said Miza.

"Then can I kill him?"

"Shut up, Tia. He's going to be all right. Just don't excite him. As if you ever could."

"My engines!"

"What happened?" asked Norlin.

He forced himself upright. A stab of pain lanced through his chest. He touched the spot where a medistrip worked to heal cracked ribs.

The control room looked as if a bomb had exploded inside it. He tried to remember if the aliens had fired on them.

"The aliens did this? Or was it the asteroid exploding from our shift?"

"The shift did it. We caught a piece of rock the side of your damned head. I ought to use your skull to plug the hole. Went right through my damned drive exciter chamber."

"Are we still in shift?"

"We can't go much longer," Barse said. "We need a dry dock soon—within a few hours. Either that or a good undertaker." She snorted in disgust. "Cancel that. No undertaker. We'll need a mass spectrometer capable of counting individual atoms. There might not even be that much left of us."

Norlin got to his feet and almost passed out. Sarov grabbed him and guided him to a bench along the far bulkhead. Norlin looked for his command chair and saw it had been twisted out of shape. Severed wires and foptic cables dangled from the base.

"Get it fixed. I can't keep track of the *Preceptor* without it."

"Right away, you suicidal, murdering son of a bitch."

"That's Captain whatever-you-said."

"Right, Cap'n," agreed Barse. She used a remote control to start a half-dozen insect-sized repair robots working on the command chair. Norlin conducted a cursory examination of the remainder of the control room and didn't like what he saw.

"The asteroid exploded and a piece — several — hit us. What about the alien cruisers?"

From the way Sarov smiled he knew the answer before his tac officer replied.

"Both are space debris, Captain. We took 'em out good and proper. The *Preceptor* is on its way to becoming an ace. Three enemy vessels vacuumed, two to go and the award's all ours."

Norlin nodded curtly and instantly regretted it. The medistrip had healed his ribs rapidly with its combination of injected medicine and radiation, but the headache refused to abate. He dismissed the notion of checking Sarov's station. They needed repair, not another battle. From the condition he was in, navigation might be the full extent of his ability.

Or luck.

"Captain Norlin, I must protest," spoke up Liottey. "You are treating me like a child. I outrank you, have seniority aboard this vessel, and I am older by far."

"Senile is a better description," muttered Miza.

Liottey ignored her jibe.

"I demand to be put in charge of something significant."

"Life support systems aren't important?" asked Norlin.

He put an arm around the man's shoulders and guided him away from the others. A few minutes earnest discussion with Liottey had the executive officer beaming and eager once more.

Barse looked up from her work on the command chair.

"What the hell did you say to him? He looks like the ship's cat who just found the only mouse in fourteen light-years."

"Do we have a ship's cat?" asked Norlin. "I haven't seen it."

"Neutron is locked up below. He's got gas so bad we only let him out when there's real trouble aboard. I love to hear the gas warfare conventions negotiators protest him running loose."

"Better let him out, then. And Liottey will be all right. He'll stay out of everyone's way for a few hours. After that, it might not matter."

Norlin gingerly put the HUD on and studied the read-outs on Chikako Miza's console. He let out a deep sigh. He shifted from being caught in one plasma jet to another. The asteroid had physically damaged them too much for the *Preceptor* to continue to Sutton II. They had to drop back into normal space soon for repairs.

"Any suggestions?" he asked Miza.

The dark-haired woman turned her head sideways and touched contacts in her silver-webbed hair.

"Only one. A rebel base on Murgatroyd."

"Never heard of it," said Norlin. He had little liking for rebels, but colonies choosing not to live under the aegis of Emperor Arian were increasing. How they cut their imperial ties varied. Some rebelled, others engaged in lengthy legal battles in the emperor's own courts. Nor-lin preferred the latter course, even if took centuries.

"Heavens to Murgatroyd?" asked Barse. "I know it. We can get whatever we need there. They've got a com-plete base with an orbiting dry dock."

"What will they accept as payment? How much of a rebel base is Murgatroyd?"

"Very," admitted Barse. "But I know them." She stared at him without flinching. "That's my home planet."

Norlin accepted it without comment. How people came to the Empire Service didn't concern him. That they had useful skills and talents did. Barse had hinted at rebellious leanings before, but he had no idea how deeply committed to them she was.

"Chikako, prepare us to drop out of shift space as close to Murgatroyd as possible."

"What are you going to be doing?" the woman asked, dark eyes narrowed.

"Engineer Barse said the shift drive exciter chamber needed work. I'll help her. In my current condition, about all I'm good for is watching RRUs work. I'll double-check your navigational procedure, if you want, but I recommend you get it right so I won't be embarrassed."

He left the bridge, brain swinging in wild, crazy orbits inside his head. Norlin kept from weaving by steadying himself against a bulkhead. Any less effort would have been undignified, and a captain of a cruiser had to remain decorous at all times.

He carefully made his way aft toward the engine section, passing through the triple airlock separating the shift engines from the rest of the ship.

He simply stood and stared when he saw the damage that had been done. When Barse had said a "rock" had smashed through the exciter chamber, he had pictured something small. Reality gave him a full-meter-diameter hole.

"Really spectacular, isn't it?" Tia Barse asked. "No way my robots can get it fixed. Dry dock or nothing."

"Keep them working. If we patch it up as much as we can, it'll speed up repairs in dry dock. I don't want to stay too long in orbit around Murgatroyd. The sector base at Sutton has to know what's happening. I'm not even certain Lyman transmitted complete data on the Death Fleet."

"Just imagine them sitting there on Sutton II, fat, dumb and as happy as if they had good sense. Here comes the Death Fleet. What would they do?"

"Fight better than they did on Lyman IV, I hope," he answered. "But I suspect it would be more like Penum. Without warning, the Death Fleet would strike and easily claim another system."

Norlin tried to take his eyes off the gaping hole in the chamber wall. If that hunk of iron asteroid had gone through the *Preceptor* only ten meters forward the cruiser would have been split in half. The shift drive would have turned them into high-energy gamma rays.

"Have Miza wake me. I'll be in my quarters trying to get rid of my headache."

"What? Backing out on helping me? Sweet dreams, Cap'n," Barse called after him. "If you have any idea how to get rid of *my* headache, be sure to tell me." She pointed at the hole.

※　※　※

"That's Murgatroyd?" he asked.

The heads-up display worked sporadically, so he used the vidscreen for a magnified image of the planetary surface. Small towns dotted the land surface; sailing ships worked the oceans, leaving behind wake profiles that identified them from space. What startled him the most was the size and complexity of the Murgatroyd space station in comparison to the technology level onplanet.

"They're demanding an entry code," said Sarov. "They promise to reduce us to dust if we don't respond."

"I'll talk to them," spoke up Tia Barse. Norlin switched her into the ship's exterior lasercom link. It took almost ten minutes of argument before she told him, "They'll work on us—for a price. I had to call in a lot of markers." She made a spitting noise. "I have to see my old boyfriend. What a pig."

"What do they want from us?" Norlin worried that a world in even quiet rebellion against the Emperor might not permit the *Preceptor* to leave dock. Such a powerful vessel would augment any world's defenses.

Barse didn't answer for five heartbeats. Then she said slowly, "They want both forward laser cannons. Cap'n, I need the exciter chamber fixed or we'll never shift again."

"Very well." Norlin seethed.

Without their forward cannon, they lost a significant portion of their firepower. He cursed the need for pragmatism in the trade.

He had to reach his sector base with the data on the Death Fleet. If he had to strip the *Preceptor* down to its superstructure to accomplish his mission, he would. But it still rankled.

"They promise we'll be on our way inside ten hours."

"Ten?"

"They're good, Cap'n. I know most of them—trained some of 'em myself. And the entire dry dock is automated. They plug in and nothing holds them back."

"I'll leave these details in your capable hands, Engineer." Norlin's headache returned, and he wanted nothing more than to turn everything over to his crew. If his XO had been more capable, he might have. Gowan Liottey's lack of ability and common sense put increased burden on his shoulders.

For twelve solid hours, he watched the Murgatroyd dry dock robots ripping and tearing at the guts of his ship. Occasional computer checks against optimal repair showed a correlation of almost one. The robotic crew was everything Barse had promised.

❅ ❅ ❅

"Cap'n, can we get into space?" his engineer asked. Her eyes had dark rings under them, and she moved as if she'd been dropped on a high-g world.

"What's wrong?"

"Nothing." She smiled crookedly. "Vasily is still the man I remembered, but damn, can he wear me out fast."

Norlin took a deep breath and let it out slowly. More than the *Preceptor* had been raped to get the repairs done.

He couldn't take his eyes off the twin holes forward where the lasartillery battery had been. Still, this seemed a small price to pay—and Barse might have gotten the better of her part of the deal, too. From her satisfied expression, he could certainly believe it was true.

"All hands, all hands," he barked into his command circuit. "Prepare for full check. All circuits, all systems. When we're finished, we do a shift drive simulation for full power."

"No need, Cap'n. They already ran the specs on the new drive alignment for us. It's in the computer."

"Do it anyway." He didn't trust them. Rebels need not be violent or malicious people—while on Sutton he had met several who carried diplomatic credentials. The only point of disagreement he had found lay in how they wanted to be governed. They thought they could do better at a planetary level than Emperor Arian did from the Crystal Throne on Earth.

Sometimes, in the dark of night and deep in his heart, Norlin almost agreed. The genhanced corps surrounding the emperor often seemed cruel and capricious. Overall, though, the Empire Service existed to serve the populace and did a good job, considering the vast distances between planets.

His frown deepened when he thought of the threat facing all humanity. Worlds independent and isolated from each other had little chance of opposing the aliens. Even with the full might of the Empire Service turned against the invaders, he wasn't sure how effective they'd be. But united they had a better chance than any single planet facing the dark metal horde. That much was apparent from the destruction of both Penum and Lyman.

"Barse, Sarov," he said, a sudden thought striking him. "Have you examined the captured weapons module?"

"I have," Mitri Sarov said. "It appears functional."

"How difficult would it be to install in place of the forward lasartillery?" Norlin stared at the gaping voids where his laser cannon had been ripped out.

The tactical officer and the engineer argued for several minutes, then came to a grudging agreement about power connections, control and possible chance for disaster.

"The damned thing will blow up on us," insisted Barse. "But I'll wire it in anyway. You're a fool, Cap'n. You'll let that skin-headed son of a bitch talk you into using it, just to see what it'll do."

"I have an adequate amount of hair on my head," Sarov protested angrily.

Norlin ordered them to the stations. He continued to run full systems checks while Barse's RRUs installed the captured alien radiation cannon.

When a split image appeared in his HUD, he knew Barse had finished roughing in the weapon mount.

"Murgatroyd is demanding our departure. They are experiencing increasing unrest due to our presence," Miza reported. "I say nuke them and to hell with the whole rebel lot."

"Your opinion is noted and rejected, Sub-commander," Norlin said. He didn't want Barse starting another argument. Murgatroyd was her home. Even though they all ought to be loyal to Emperor Arian and the Empire Service, he knew better than to let one officer insult another's home world.

"All systems are operating, most at minimum acceptable levels," he announced. "Let's oblige our hosts and get into space. Prepare for undocking from Murgatroyd station."

He watched the summary displays parade by in his HUD, taking some satisfaction that the flickering had been repaired, appreciating how well the crew worked together when they weren't arguing.

"Excellent," he said. "Course laid in for Sutton II. Set alarm to sound when we are at a distance acceptable for using shift engines."

They had just spiraled out and applied power to the ion engines to get up to shift speed when Miza and Sarov both yelled for his attention.

"Report in summary." He watched the data jerk across his field of vision from both officers.

"We've got six missiles incoming," barked the tactical officer.

"We've got range and position on the ship launching them."

"Evasive action," he ordered. Norlin shuddered as the *Preceptor* dodged and cast out defensive ECM missiles to confuse or intercept the six missiles seeking them. With the forward lasartillery gone, their defensive capacity was diminished significantly.

"What do we do, Cap'n?" asked Barse. "Do we run or fight?"

Norlin leaned back in the command chair and studied the readouts before making a decision. He reached out and touched a single button.

Chapter Nine

"Cap'n, you've killed power to the engines. I need it to run!" shrieked Barse. Norlin had never heard the woman so agitated.

"Prepare the alien radiation cannon for use," he ordered. "Full power to it, Engineer. Is it properly patched into the weapons computer, Tactical Officer?"

"Aye, Captain," came Sarov's bull-throated reply. "I put an interpreter circuit online to translate voltage levels. I think I have them matched." Sarov waited for a moment, then asked, "You're not trusting the damned alien popgun, are you?"

"I am."

Pier Norlin had looked at the readouts from the weapons computer and the main systems. The *Preceptor* had power enough to shift but lacked the peak energy requirements for battle. The sensors reported the rebel craft to be bristling with laser turrets. Some might be for show, but he thought otherwise. The approaching flight of genius missiles told him the rebel craft was armed to the teeth and meant to cripple rather than destroy.

They wanted salvage, and the cruiser's crew would only be a hindrance to efficient looting.

"They think we blew the main power bus," reported Miza. "I've tapped into their intercom — it isn't properly shielded. They're saying something about sabotage in the dock."

"I'll have Vasily's balls for more than..." Barse's voice trailed off as she fumed. Norlin heard the engineer ripping into recently repaired circuits. She would find the sabotage device quickly enough now that she looked. He left her to the chore. He had a ship to defend.

"Miza, are they suspicious?"

"They think their gizmo did us in."

"Prepare the alien cannon. Dead on, no warning, no quarter." The command burned his tongue, but this wasn't a civil engagement. This was war. Worse, it was sabotage and ambush.

Norlin wanted to scream in the silence that descended on the control room. No one moved, no one breathed. The silence made him start to mutter to himself to break it.

Then all hell broke loose.

Norlin blanked his summary displays except for the weapons computer. He gasped when he saw the huge number of burned-out circuits. Then the high-pitched screech started.

"Air leak. We've got a punctured hull. Liottey, tend to it. Now, dammit, do it now!"

Norlin monitored the pressure drop and saw it was minor. He isolated it in the forward mounts where the lasartillery had been. Firing the radiation cannon had cracked portions of the composite material hull — nothing serious. It could be patched with glue.

"Report, all stations!" he barked.

Before the first status report came in, the lights went off.

"What happened?" he demanded.

He ripped off his dead HUD and tossed it aside. From behind him, in the control room, he heard Miza and Sarov cursing as they worked. Not even the emergency lighting had come on. "Power to the lighting. Do it, Liottey."

"Done, Captain." And it was.

The emergency lights were designed to fill the bridge with harsh white light. They cast wan beams. Since that was far from the proper illumination level, Norlin knew their batteries were run down. He would have a talk with the XO about this. Later.

"Getting a trickle of power back. Barse is manually switching."

"Was it the rebel's sabotage device that did it?"

"It was an aftereffect of the radiation cannon," came Sarov's surprising answer. "It set up a field, sent the beam, then a secondary field sucked up power to recharge. All power, even from batteries and fuel cells not connected to it. We hadn't expected it to cycle like that."

"Get us back to power. Liottey, how bad is the rupture in the hull?"

"Almost fixed, Captain Norlin," came the XO's thin voice. "A robot repair unit is working now. It's lucky the RRUs don't need light to work. I can hardly see where I am."

"I'll send you a flashlight and a pair of hands," grumbled Norlin. "Maybe you can find your—"

"Cap'n, power's coming back at half-level."

"Thanks, Engineer."

Norlin slid the command visor back on and checked the summary displays. The ship had been dead in space for several minutes, but it hadn't mattered. The alien's radiation cannon had been centered on the rebel ship. It now drifted, a lifeless husk, across the Murgatroyd system.

"It's dead," came Miza's appraisal. "All internals are gone. The radiation cooked 'em alive, the sons of bitches.

That'll teach the rebels to run a sneak attack on the *Preceptor*!"

"Enough," he snapped.

Barse had grown up on Murgatroyd. Friends might have been aboard the attacking ship. He didn't need dissension among his crew when they were faced with monumental problems.

He watched in the HUD as his crew worked to restore order. Less than fifteen minutes after the power level had come back to three-quarters, Miza exclaimed, "I'll be sucked into a black hole. They're on top of us!"

"The rebel ship? You said it was dead."

"Not the rebel. It's history. The aliens. A scoutship just shifted into the system. I think it's locked onto us. It's vectoring in on us, using a least-time orbit. They want us bad. They're not making any attempt at stealth approach."

Norlin popped up Miza's full display and saw the readouts. Her personality might be closer to a viper than a human, but Chikako Miza knew her job. She had spotted the alien scout seconds after it shifted out of FTL drive.

"Can we hide behind the rebel ship?" he asked. "Grapple and drift, as if we were part of it?"

"No good," came Sarov's evaluation. "The scout has us dead in its sights. We can't do anything clever now without it jumping down our throats."

"We're still in the Murgatroyd gravitational well," said Miza. "Any chance we can get back to the station? This is as much their problem as ours."

Norlin nodded. An alien scout meant others followed. The Death Fleet cared little which world it struck; to it, human politics were irrelevant. A rebel planet meant as much in the way of plunder as a world firmly supporting Emperor Arian.

He tried a lasercom back to Murgatroyd and got only static. A quick check showed he lacked the comlink power required to drive a beam through the alien's interference.

"It's being mistaken for natural static," said Miza. "We can send back a message packet."

"Forget it. Murgatroyd has to solve its own problems. It won't do us any good dying for them. We've got to get the warning to Sutton II and the Empire Service."

"The alien is on an intercept course. They either have extremely sensitive detectors or they're homing on a beacon."

"The radiation cannon?" Norlin had never considered the possibility that the aliens keyed each weapons module to a ship and could track any wayward pieces. "Liottey, check out the cannon for transmitters. The alien is tracking us too easily."

He didn't wait for his exec officer's whining voice to complain about the chore interfering with his other duties. He switched to Miza's display and studied the surrounding region of the Murgatroyd system. They hadn't blasted long enough to get far from the main planet.

"Tia, how many moons around Murgatroyd?"

"Two, Cap'n. Both are small but big enough to put down on if you're careful."

"I'm more desperate than careful. Prepare for maneuvering. We're going to put some rock between us and the alien and see if they *are* homing on their cannon."

The *Preceptor* slowly swung about as he gingerly applied power to the jets. The ship responded poorly; Norlin fought it all the way down to a hard landing on the surface of the outermost moon. He cringed when he saw the number of new danger indicator lights flaring in front of him. He toggled the problems over to Liottey.

His full attention turned to signals from a small sensor he had left along their flight path. Using it, he monitored the progress of the alien scoutship.

"It might have been bad luck on our part being between shift-out and Murgatroyd," ventured Miza. "The scout isn't paying us much attention."

Norlin checked the progress of the repair work. The RRUs toiled to fix the hull, to repair the short-circuited equipment, to do a dozen things necessary for a successful and reasonably safe shift. In its present condition, the *Preceptor* was neither fight nor flight worthy.

"Sarov, prepare a few missiles. We'll have to use them instead of the radiation cannon. We can't get back to power fast enough, no matter how effective the device is."

"Permission to launch a nuke at Murgatroyd, Captain," requested Sarov.

"What?" came Barse's aggrieved protest. "What's that bald son of a bitch think he's doing? He can't fire on them. That was a pirate ship. The people on Murgatroyd or the station had nothing to do with it."

"Quiet down," Norlin ordered. Even knowing there had been sabotage done at Murgatroyd station to set them up for the attack did not blip on her convictions. She was loyal to Murgatroyd and ignored evidence.

The engineer continued her tirade against Sarov, his ancestors and their scurrilous, disgusting personal habits.

"Explain," he ordered his tactical officer as he muted Barse's vituperation to a low, angry buzz.

"They're alert for such an attack. They'll pick up the incoming missile and respond to destroy it. They'll also look for the source. This is the only way I can think to get their attention focused on the alien scoutship."

"And the Death Fleet. Murgatroyd's cometary detectors might be circumvented by now," said Norlin. His mind raced. Launching an attack on the planet had other advantages. It might get the alien scout's attention and force it to turn tail and run.

"Launch," he ordered.

He switched to Barse's circuit and worked to calm her, explaining his line of reasoning. She quieted, but he knew her anger had not abated.

"It's not right. People could die."

"If a few die now, it might save the entire world. You saw what the Death Fleet did to Lyman IV." Norlin's throat tightened as he thought of Neela.

"You might be right," Barse conceded with ill-grace.

"It's Sarov's idea. I only approved it. Tia," he said in a lower voice. "The *Preceptor* is a crew. We're all working for the same thing. None of us wants to see the aliens wash over humanity like a tidal wave."

The ship hummed as the missile launched along the magnetic rails. Norlin shifted to Miza's readouts and watched the nuke race away. He was more interested in the scoutship's response than in Murgatroyd's reaction.

"That spooked them," he said. "The scout is spinning around and getting out of here. Put a tracer on it, Miza. I don't want it to slip off where we can't find it."

"Captain, I found a transmission device in the cannon. What should I do with it?"

"Any booby trap on it?"

"I don't think so."

"Be sure, then remove the device and destroy it."

"Wait, Captain. Let me have it. We might learn more about their com capability."

"Very well. Give it to Miza after you're sure it's not dangerous. Are the air leaks fixed?"

"Yes, sir. All done. I used—"

He cut off Liottey's long-winded description of how he had repaired the breached hull. The details mattered less than knowing the job had been completed. Norlin had too many other things on his mind to care a pinch of space dust about glues and patches.

He blinked, got a new view on the HUD and saw their missile enter the Murgatroyd detection net. Indicators flashed at the clumsy attack, and interception came quickly.

"Can we get a comlink with Murgatroyd yet?" he asked Miza.

"Negative, Captain. The scout is still blanketing us. I wish I knew how they did it. All channels are garbled. We might as well be in the middle of a major proton storm."

"Send a warning packet to Murgatroyd," he ordered Sarov. "Give them the details on our sensor readings on the scout."

"Major shift-out," Miza said. "Hundreds—thousands! The Death Fleet is in the system."

Norlin slumped. He picked up more details of the Murgatroyd defensive system. They had been alerted by the single missile. Otherwise, they would have been caught as unaware as the Penum system and Lyman IV, for all the advance knowledge of the Death Fleet the latter had been given.

He didn't need Miza to tell him the aliens' attack came immediately.

"It's all elbows and assholes down there," said Barse. "I've got us up to ninety percent power."

"What about the radiation cannon?"

"Can't use it, Cap'n. Not unless you want to cripple us permanently. I've got to run a second power line to it for its recharge cycle. Otherwise, it'll use a secondary energy field to suck us drier than—"

"Thank you, Engineer."

He prayed that enough systems worked well enough to allow them to shift. If they remained on the moon that had briefly given them shelter, they would become easy prey for the Death Fleet's heavy radiation cannon. Their only chance for survival now was to sneak off.

"Murgatroyd is responding," Miza reported. "They've launched deep space interceptors. Monitoring their com, Captain. It's interesting. What to snoop in?"

Norlin keyed into the rebel world's internal communication. A brief smile crossed his lips. They thought the Empire Service attacked. The first missile had been identified as ES make and this mobilized their defense quickly. Only time would tell if they fought with enough fervor and strength to hold back the black tide of alien death.

"Got one on us. A destroyer from its size."

"Shift. Can we shift?" he asked.

"Deploying doggo missiles in addition to actives. We can hold it at bay for a few minutes. That ought to be long enough to get us far enough away from the moon for a shift."

Norlin put the *Preceptor* on a vector that made it difficult for the destroyer to center its radiation cannon on the fleeing ship. He had learned enough of the weapons configurations to know where their best chance lay.

"We can't shift, Captain. Too many backup systems are down."

"Hit the primary systems and give me a prayer. We're leaving Murgatroyd now."

Norlin saw the pre-discharge corona building in the destroyer just as his finger toggled the shift button. They might have been too close to the moon. The destroyer might have closed at the last moment and come within their shift field. Norlin neither knew nor cared. They had no time to waste.

The *Preceptor* entered shift space just as a powerful wavefront buffeted them.

Chapter Ten

Norlin worked to activate as many robot repair units as possible. From his summary display, he saw that both Barse and Liottey directed their tireless RRUs personally rather than allowing the AI devices to operate on their own. He doubted Liottey's selections for repair were as timely as Barse's, but he did not bother the XO to inquire. Everything needed repair aboard the *Preceptor*. The shift had damaged many major circuits and most minor ones.

"Give me a playback on the last few seconds before shift," he ordered Miza. "I want to know what blew up behind us."

"It wasn't the pursuing alien vessel," said Sarov. "But something of major proportions did explode. Heavy radiation up and down the spectrum. Lots of gamma. The EMP damaged my combat sensors."

"Got it," said Miza.

Norlin ran the playback on the control room vidscreen. The moon hadn't exploded from their shift field, nor had the attacking alien destroyer. The Death Fleet had met unexpected resistance on Murgatroyd and had unleashed a weapon of fearsome power.

The entire planet had been obliterated.

"Analysis," Norlin ordered in a choked voice. "I want full specs on it before we reach Sutton II. Our report is going to be as complete as we can make it."

"They didn't leave anything to plunder. The whole damned world is gone," cried Barse.

"If they can't sneak up on us, they'll use overwhelming force. They must be terrified that we can mount a good defense and destroy them," said Sarov.

"They're aliens. Who can say how they think?" Chikako Miza's usually cynical tone was muted by shock.

"They destroyed the whole goddamn planet!"

Barse's wail filled the ship. Norlin groped for the words that would soothe her, but he found nothing. How did anyone make the pain of a world's death go away? He had yet to accept Neela Cosarrian's death and make it less grievous. He thought the pain might never fade—how did he ease Barse's over an entire planet?

"I'm getting a danger indication on the exciter chamber, Engineer. I thought you fixed it."

"It was working fine. The hole was properly patched, Cap'n."

"Not according to my readouts. Do your job, Barse."

Norlin heard her curse him and then cut the connection. He rubbed his ear where the rice-grain-sized receiver rested. She knew how to curse and had done a good job of it, missing nothing in his ancestry or personal habits. He hoped his spurious order kept her busy and took her away from her more immediate grief. He wondered if Vasily had meant as much to her as Neela had to him.

"Does everyone have something to do?" He checked the summary on his heads-up display and saw the reds slowly fade to ambers in some cases, blues in others and 100-percent-functional green in the rest. The *Preceptor*'s crew worked hard to get things shipshape again.

"Good," he said, climbing out of his command chair. He felt as if he had become a part of it—and it had grafted onto him. Stretching, he knew there wasn't a great deal he could do at the moment. He piloted, he navigated, he commanded.

And he was so tired that walking presented problems. He wobbled a bit and supported himself against a bulkhead. No one noticed—they were too engrossed in directing repair units and running computer maintenance programs. Norlin straightened, composed himself and left the bridge, being certain to take his small belt comlink with him. A few hours sleep would revive him enough not to make critical errors. If anyone required him in the meantime, they could summon him on the 'link.

He collapsed on the pneumatic bed in the spacious captain's quarters and snored loudly within minutes.

❄ ❄ ❄

"It'll have to do," Norlin said with some regret. He had wanted to bring the *Preceptor* in to the Sutton II sector base with 100 percents in all systems. Reality had intruded after the second week in shift space.

Barse lacked the heavy equipment needed to overhaul the engines and re-tune them. They were almost past tolerance for shift; another few millionths of a radian out of synchronization, and the ship would require extensive dry-dock refitting and calibration.

If the misalignment did not destroy them first.

The statistics about shift space disasters were always on his mind. Slipping along the multi-dimensional membranes was closer to art than science, and he was the only artist/scientist aboard allowed to make decisions.

"This isn't the Inspector General's review, Captain," complained Miza. "We're lucky to be alive and have information. They don't know what the Death Fleet can do."

"They don't even know *of* the Death Fleet," cut in Barse. "Considering how tangled in bureaucracy they are at sector, it might be a year before anyone even reads our report."

"I'm reporting as far up the chain of command as I can," said Norlin.

"That's likely to be the door attendant," Miza said, sneering. "Who's going to listen to a sub-lieutenant?"

"I'm captain of a line vessel," Norlin said coldly. He was acutely aware of his low rank and lack of standing. At a sector base, they used sub-lieutenants to run errands, not trusting them with important tasks. In the eyes of the senior officers, they were hardly more than ensigns who had a year's experience behind them.

He thought back to the incredible odyssey he had undertaken. The research ship duty had been important for investigating dark matter interaction with the higher dimension membranes that determined physical laws. The scout's message about Penum had ripped him away from the dull routine and thrust him into a vortex that refused to stop whirling. From research ship to captain of an Empire Service cruiser via command of Lyman IV's major space station in hours was unprecedented in ES history.

To his credit, he had fought off an alien scoutship and retrieved a weapons module containing their fearsome radiation cannon, had shifted into another battle and won then eluded the Death Fleet's hunter-killers before the total destruction of Murgatroyd. It had been an eventful few weeks.

And then there was Neela. His thoughts kept returning to her frail, emaciated body. Starvation and imprisonment had worn on her, but she should have survived. He had arrived in time. There wasn't any reason for her to have perished—unless it was his fault. Over and over, he blamed himself, even though he knew it was self-destructive folly.

Norlin shook himself out of the reverie and toggled on the laser comlink to base.

"ES Cruiser *Preceptor* requesting emergency docking. Triple-A priority claimed."

"That's the wrong priority," cut in Miza. "We're a Nova Class cruiser. Try A-Double-Z."

"A-Double-Z priority claimed."

The headphone crackled with static. "What is this, amateurs on tour?"

"No vidshow," he replied. "Need immediate clearance to dock and to see the sector commandant. Highly classified material, partially analyzed, requires full eyes-only attention."

"You need full attention — in a whackatorium. You *are* in a cruiser, but I have it under the command of Captain Dukker. Who the hell are you?"

"Norlin. Dukker is dead. I cannot discuss this matter, even on a laser link."

"Then go play with yourself. You're seventeenth in the landing sequence."

"Let me use the radiation cannon to clear a path. That will get their attention," said Sarov.

"That'll get us blown out of the sky," snapped Norlin. To the clearance controller, he said, "Let me speak with the duty officer."

"I'll let you speak with the provost. You need to be locked up before you run loose and hurt yourself."

The vidscreen flickered once. The display showed a straight-nosed, stern-looking sub-commander. He cleared his throat, glared then asked, "Where is Dukker?"

"Dead by misadventure. He was killed during a mutiny on the Lyman IV station. The entire world is gone."

"What do you mean gone? If this is a joke, you're all going to spend a hundred years at hard labor on a prison world."

"We have full documentation of the complete occupation and looting or destruction of three planets. The

Empire has lost the Penum, Lyman and Murgatroyd systems."

"Murgatroyd rebelled," snorted the sub-commander. "What's this about the other two worlds?"

Norlin macroburst-transmitted the dead scout's data about Penum then added everything they had recorded during orbit around Lyman IV. The summary startled the other officer. His eyes widened, and he licked thin lips with the tip of his tongue.

"These look real. The time marks, the official encoding..."

"They're real. We have further documentation on the Death Fleet and Murgatroyd's complete destruction. The aliens looted Penum and Lyman. They blew the whole damned planet of Murgatroyd apart."

"Impossible."

Norlin transmitted it and took cold comfort in the officer's response.

"If I hadn't witnessed it, I would have doubted it was possible, too. Emperor Arian's strategists said it wasn't possible to blow up a world like that. The aliens just proved that it is."

"You have full coverage?"

"As complete as a cruiser's sensors can furnish."

The sub-commander's face turned into an impassive mask. Norlin saw the man's facial muscles twitch occasionally and guessed that a higher-level officer was being summoned.

"I'm Captain Droon," came a graying officer's introduction. "Dock immediately. We have a tug to facilitate. Report to my office at once upon docking, Captain. You and your entire crew."

"Yes, sir," Norlin agreed. He leaned back and wiped a forehead drenched with sweat. "We got through to someone. Does anyone know who he is?"

"Droon? He's station commandant," supplied Liottey. "An excellent officer. He—"

"Never mind. I'll find out his good points when we report. Everyone have a full memory bar for Captain Droon's analysis. No holding back." Norlin sat back and rubbed his chin as he thought. He added, "Keep copies aboard ship for later use." He turned off the intercom and stood.

A tiny beep interrupted his departure for the airlock. He switched to the private circuit with Tia Barse.

"What is it, Engineer?"

"You want to turn over the radiation cannon to them?"

"Of course. It's a vital factor in defeating the Death Fleet. If we nullify their weapons, they're crippled and vulnerable. Even if we can't defend, we can duplicate. It's a hell of an efficient weapon."

"Hold back on reporting it, Cap'n. Just until you see how the meeting goes. You already asked us to keep copies of our reports and all data."

Norlin considered the full ramifications of what she said. He had seen the tangles and missed chances and fouled-up decisions made by the Empire Service during his cadet training at the academy. It might be no worse than any other military branch throughout history, but the inadequacies seemed to be magnified by the immense distances between stars.

On the frontier, several hundred light-years from Earth and Emperor Arian's court, procedures were looser and accountability difficult to achieve. Revealing the installed radiation cannon later in no way violated his oath to support the Empire. If anything, it aided the Empire by making his initial presentation simple.

"All right. What do the others say about it?" he asked Barse.

"They agree. All four of us."

This surprised him. He had expected another round of bitter dispute, especially with Liottey. The foppish executive officer seldom agreed with the others.

He popped the cerampix memory bars from the computer and motioned for Sarov and Miza to precede him off the ship. He wanted a last look at the bridge. Now that they had reached sector headquarters, he would no longer command such a fine ship. With luck and an impressive enough presentation to Captain Droon, he might get a first officer's berth on a smaller vessel. Even an Empire Service destroyer was a major promotion over a research picket ship.

But no destroyer could match the *Preceptor*.

He turned smartly and marched out. The docking had been done without his supervision, and human inspectors rushed aboard to check out completely the damaged systems. Norlin hesitated when he heard a sharp order recalling the inspectors. They milled around, then left the ship.

"Robot crews only," came the order. "Captain Droon wants to lead the inspection team himself."

Norlin smiled wanly. His report wasn't going to be ignored, not when the station commandant attended to it personally.

He and the others marched in silence, each wrapped in thought. They stopped in front of the commandant's door, and Norlin paused to take a deep, settling breath then touched the acceptor plate. The brightly painted security door slid open with a faint metallic hiss. He entered stiffly.

"Sub-Lieutenant Norlin reporting as ordered, sir."

A snickering from the side of the room caused him to sneak a quick sidelong look. A man dressed in a rumpled captain's uniform sat on the floor, long, apelike arms around his drawn-up knees. From the way he shook, he fought to keep from laughing hysterically.

"Memory bars. On the desk."

The deep voice brought Norlin back to the officer seated behind the furniture alluded to. Dashes of distinguished gray in his hair told of long experience. The strong lines of his jaw and the cold eyes made Norlin shiver. Captain Droon was a man accustomed to giving orders and having them obeyed instantly.

Norlin and the others placed their cerampix bars on the desk. Droon scooped them up and dropped them into a viewer. He dumped the contents into the station computer before turning back.

"This has been transmitted to headquarters on-planet. Admiral Bendo has been summoned and will examine the documents personally. I have recommended a full staff meeting after he has time to study the data."

"Thank you, sir," said Norlin.

"Well done, all of you. Your summaries give me the feeling you've all performed admirably. I'm recommending class-two citations for each of you."

"Just what we need," muttered Miza. "Now I can die happy."

Norlin motioned her to silence. She glared at him.

Another bout of laughter, this time touching demoniacal limits, came from the officer sitting on the floor.

"Sir...?" started Norlin. He had too much to report and had so little time.

"I know you've been under a strain. Thank you for taking Captain Dukker's post. Sorry thing, rebellion. Dukker is recommended for an Empire Star."

"He gets a decoration, and all we get is a checkmark on our records?" blurted Barse.

"Correct, Engineer. I'm sure he died nobly. Dukker was a favorite of Emperor Arian."

"He was—"

Norlin cut her off before she told Droon her opinion of their former captain.

"Captain Pensky is now in command of the *Preceptor*. He is a third cousin to the emperor and highly qualified for such a post. Sub-Lieutenant, you will act as advisor until the captain is familiar with the ship."

Droon motioned to the man sitting on the floor, who scuttled on hands and knees and slithered up the side of the desk like a snake.

"It's mine? You're giving me the cruiser?" the man said.

"Go on a shakedown patrol, Pavel. Learn everything you can of the cruiser's operation. We'll need you soon, if this young officer's report on what he calls the Death Fleet is accurate."

"I can do anything I want with the ship? Oh, this is going to be fun!" Captain Pensky skipped from the room, leaving Norlin staring openmouthed at him.

"Again, officers, I am proud to acknowledge your loyalty. Please aid your new captain in whatever way you can. Dismissed."

"Captain Droon," said Norlin. "*He* is in charge?"

"Pavel? Of course. He is highly regarded by the emperor and his court. You can learn a great deal from him. He's a brilliant tactician and was top-rated by the emperor in last year's Imperial War Games competition."

"He's genhanced?"

"Of course." Droon's cold eyes turned colder. "Report back to the *Preceptor* immediately. You are under Captain Pensky's command. Dismissed."

❊ ❊ ❊

Norlin stood outside the station commandant's office, unable to speak without choking on his indignation. Gales of insane laughter echoed back along the corridor from the direction of the stairwell leading to the docks.

"And I thought *Dukker* was a null," said Miza. She cast a glance at Norlin then walked off, head high and arrogant. Liottey and Sarov trailed after her like captive satellites.

"Yeah," said Barse, "and I thought *you* were a null, too. Live and learn." She stalked off, shoulders hunched and eyes fixed on the dull-surfaced composite deck as if she might find something cheering there.

Pier Norlin returned to the *Preceptor* in a daze. Even as a lower-rank cadet, he had more command ability than Captain Pavel Pensky.

But he wasn't genhanced—or the emperor's favorite cousin.

Chapter Eleven

"Make certain there are plenty of genius missiles in the magazine," said the *Preceptor*'s new captain. "I want to shoot things."

Pavel Pensky jumped onto the command chair and put his feet on the bottom pneumatic cushion. He wrapped his impossibly long arms around his doubled knees and rocked forward.

Norlin watched in astonishment. The genhanced officer's balance was nothing less than superb. He wished he could make that claim about any other aspect of the man's behavior. Turning over such a powerful ship to a madman might mean their deaths.

"Full armament, Captain," announced Sarov. "All munitions loaded." The burly tactical officer didn't seem uneasy at the irrational way Pensky acted.

Norlin tried to put his fears into perspective. He had seen many genhanced officers during his five years at the Empire Service Academy. He had thought all were strange, some eccentric and the rest completely irrational. Those few who seemed to have lost all contact with reality proved themselves the most brilliant in simulated combat tests. One of the saner instruction officers claimed they had no distractions to complicate their decisions. They saw the kernel of the problem and solved it.

Pensky might prove to be one of the genetically altered tactical geniuses. Norlin still wished he knew how the captain had been re-engineered. It might give him some insight—and faith—in the man's abilities.

"Can I fire them yet?" Pensky called out. He hadn't bothered to don the HUD command visor with its summary displays of the major systems.

"Let's leave the station first," suggested Miza. She glanced at Norlin and shrugged, as if saying *Everyone has their quirks.*

Norlin found a dropseat in the corner of the bridge and sat down to observe, since he had nothing else to do. Pensky fired off orders, most of which sounded legitimate. The few that weren't could have been jokes to ease the tension—or they might have been stark, raving madness. The crew ignored those and concentrated on the reasonable orders.

"Ready to launch. What are we heading out to do, Captain?" asked Miza.

"Nothing! Everything! I don't know. We're being invaded. We have to fight our way out. I knew it would happen. I told Arian we should put up a big wall around Earth."

"A wall of sensors? Or warships?"

"Brick! I wanted it to be brick. Fang wire isn't good enough. Too easy to get through. They can sneak under when your back is turned. Let's launch and go after them!"

Pensky expertly guided the *Preceptor* from dock and spun the ship on its axis. A small, expert application of power, a precession to get into position; and then the cruiser leaped with sudden acceleration that pinned Norlin to the poorly cushioned seat.

He marveled at Pensky's ability to control the vessel without using the command visor. How did he know where they blasted without constant update information?

Norlin had never heard of a genhanced officer with telepathic powers, although such were rumored and he remembered long hours at the academy disproving this possibility mathematically. Still, Bell's Inequality explained action at a distance—the emergency quantum interference beacon depended on faraway action. If two atoms could be quantum linked, it might be possible for telepathy to exist.

But what brand of telepathy was it that would allow Pensky to control the cruiser without once referring to the torrents of data from the equipment?

The most obvious worry Norlin had was how Captain Pensky knew where they travelled. The space around a major base was filled with traffic and presented considerable approach and departure problems for controllers.

"We're finally free of sector control and on our own," came Liottey's voice.

"And they're madder than hell, too," spoke up Miza. "We almost collided with an incoming Earther freighter loaded with electronics."

"Main engine shutdown," bellowed Barse over the all-stations comlink. "Shut the damned jets down or we'll blow up!"

"After them! They're everywhere. We can take them. I'm braver than any thousand of the swine!"

Pensky stood in the command chair and waved his arms around like a rotary blade fan. Norlin felt part of the human-created air current brush across his face and evaporate the nervous sweat beading there. On take-off, Pensky hadn't known where he vectored; he had simply cast away from the dock and ordered the ship out at random. They might have collided with any number of vessels. Norlin closed his eyes and tried not to think about madness trumping telepathy as an answer for the new captain's behavior.

"Shut down the goddamn engines!" roared Tia Barse. The engineer stood in front of the command chair and shoved her scowling face within a centimeter of Pensky's. "I don't want to end up a flash of plasma because some brain-burned cousin of the goddamn emperor wants to get his rocks off!"

"Barse! You're talking mutiny." Gowan Liottey had followed her in and stood nervously by the door to the control room. "Hush. It's not that bad."

"It is. Every light on my panel is red. I need to shut down and repair or the whole damned ship is going to explode. Do I make myself clear?" She shoved her chin out truculently and stopped it just a hair short of colliding with Pensky's.

"Engineer Barse, how nice to see you. Would you care for a spot of green tea? It's so difficult finding anyone who drinks the refined beverage out here on the frontier. Such an ugly place."

"What?" Barse stepped back and stared.

"The cha-no-yu tea ceremony. It is the rage at court. Even the emperor is learning the complete ritual. It's ancient and ever so complicated. None of the commoners learn it. That makes it so much more delicious."

"What's this got to do with my damned engines?"

"Take tea with me, and I'll order them turned off or whatever it was you wanted."

"I'd walk through hell barefoot to put them right."

Barse glanced at Norlin. He nodded. He'd see what could be done while she drank tea with the captain.

Norlin left the bridge and made his way to the engine room. On the way, he stopped and let out the ship's cat from the mess hall. The black feline with white back paws and chin whiskers stared up at him, yowled and pranced off toward the engine room, tail high. Norlin followed.

"You're the only one left on board with any sense," he told the cat. "You don't want anything to do with this crew of madmen."

The cat jumped up and perched on a wrist-thick superconducting cable feeding power into the drive engine's exciter chamber. Norlin's nose wrinkled, and he backed away.

"Barse said you had gas. I didn't realize she meant it literally."

He warily skirted the methane-releasing feline and studied the engineering board. A few minutes work at the computer console showed major problems developing. Barse hadn't been out of line demanding immediate engine shutdown. Whatever had been done to the ship in dock at Sutton, decent repairwork had not been part of it. They had received better at Murgatroyd.

Norlin was something of a perfectionist and reran the checks. He shook his head. If the *Preceptor* tried to shift, it would simply vanish in a puff of vapor. Trying to jet about inside the Sutton system seemed even riskier. He saw a dozen places where fuel leaks had developed and sent cryogenic temperature sprays into the main compartment.

He struggled with the engineering computer and summoned several RRUs from other parts of the ship, making sure he didn't take any from duty on the life support system. For once, Liottey had allocated resources well. An hour of hard work later, Norlin had metal crews repairing the most obvious problems.

"Good, you got most of them," said Barse as she joined him. "I feel better having you on board. You've got more sense in your little finger than he has in his whole goddamn head." She reached over and scooped up the fat black cat from his perch. "I see you let Neutron out. He's my secret way back."

"How's that?"

"If we run out of fuel, I'll hook his ass up to a hose and run it directly into the fuel-mixing chamber. A spark for ignition and whoosh! we're on our way home with a limitless methane supply."

"What do you feed him?"

"Whatever he wants to eat. He's an independent son of a mouser."

"Cut back on the protein," advised Norlin.

"You sound as if you've had experience. You don't strike me as the feline fancier type of officer." Barse stared hard at him.

"Just goes to show how wrong you can be."

They returned to repairing all that had been neglected back at sector base. The *Preceptor* might carry a full complement of genius missiles, but it lacked the ability to deliver them reliably.

After six hours, Norlin called a halt to the work.

"What else is there?" he asked.

"Nothing the robots can't handle on their own, Cap'n," Barse said.

He looked at her and shook his head sadly. He liked being called captain, but he no longer had any real position aboard the *Preceptor*. He was supposed to advise Pensky, but the genhanced officer had ideas of his own.

At least, he hoped the new captain had ideas. From the erratic way Pensky commanded, it was difficult to decide if there were any sane purpose to his orders.

"I'd better see how we're doing," he told the engineer.

"Norlin."

Their eyes locked for a moment.

"Go see what Captain Crazy is up to."

He smiled crookedly, nodded and left the engine room. His knowledge of the shift engine was limited but greater than anyone else's aboard ship except for Barse. Likewise, he knew more about each system than anyone but the officer in charge.

He couldn't operate the weapons computer with Sarov's flair, but he could keep the ship from being destroyed. His abilities in life support matched Liottey's — he had been in training for executive officer before deciding command pilot suited him better.

Of all the positions, he knew the least about what it took to work Chikako Miza's station. He vowed to bone up on communications and detection. With Pensky in charge, he would have the spare time.

He slid through the shielding baffles leading to the bridge and stopped just inside the hatch. Pandemonium reigned. It took him several seconds to understand that the *Preceptor* was at full battle alert—and that Mitri Sarov worked to load missiles for firing.

"Who's attacking? The Death Fleet?" he called across to Miza. She shook her head. He had never seen her so pale.

"Please, Captain Pensky," she pleaded. "It is giving all the proper recognition signals. It's one of ours!"

"It's been taken over by the aliens. Trust me. I know. It's an enemy ship. Tactical Officer, fire a full barrage. Complete spectrum of missiles. Get the forward lasartillery ready for use. They'll come for us if we miss."

"Captain," pleaded Miza, "that's *our* destroyer. We can't fire on our own vessel. It's the ES *Montgomery*, out of Sutton. IFF confirms it."

"She's right, Captain." Sarov swung around at his station. "I'm receiving counter-lock signals. They know we've homed in on them and are decoupling. The destroyer is friendly and trying hard to keep us from firing."

Pensky's finger stabbed down on a button at the edge of his command chair. The *Preceptor* hummed as one flight of missiles fired and the auto-loaders slammed replacements into the magnetic rail launchers.

"An enemy! It's an enemy!"

"We're getting recall notice from sector base, Captain. They're waving us off the destroyer."

"Don't listen. It's an alien trick. They know everything about our communication techniques. I told Droon we should have changed our recognition codes. They know everything about us!"

Norlin looked helplessly from the ranting captain to Sarov and Miza. He had no standing on the ship. He had been assigned to advise and nothing else.

But they had fired on a friendly ship.

Both Miza and Sarov would not mistake an alien craft. They'd never hesitate if they did. Now, both moved indecisively as Pensky did their work from the command chair.

"Captain," came Miza's wail. "Base says they'll declare us outlaw and order the fleet after us if we do not break off the attack immediately on the *Montgomery*."

"Lies! They're tricking us." His finger worked across the toggles for the forward lasartillery. When it failed to fire he screamed and sent out another flight of missiles.

"Direct hit," came Sarov's hollow voice. "We scored a complete destruct on the destroyer. There's not a speck of dust left."

"Sir," Miza reported, "base has ordered four cruisers and a battleship to intercept us and…"

"Blow us out of space," finished Sarov. "I picked up the same message on my classified frequency lasercom to base. Sir, we just killed a friendly—and now we're the target!"

Pier Norlin went cold inside with shock. Captain Pavel Pensky had turned them into an outlaw ship slated for destruction in less than a day on patrol.

Chapter Twelve

Pier Norlin took the command visor Pensky had discarded and donned it. He winced when the HUD revealed what the genhanced officer had done.

Sarov's summary displays showed the full weapons systems on the *Preceptor* and their status. Sixteen expensive genius missiles had struck the ill-fated destroyer; Sarov could be proud of an eighty-percent hit rate. According to the playbacks, the destroyer had deployed every countermeasure possible, to no avail. The *Preceptor* had proven too powerful and Pensky too clever.

Norlin sat on the dropseat and shook. He couldn't tell if the skillful attack had been so deadly because of superior power or expertise. What commander expected a friendly ship to open fire?

"A small sweep-fleet is closing on us, Captain," came Miza's frightened voice. "Should I send the recognition response and surrender?"

"No! They're all aliens. This is a ruse. They'll blow us out of space if you try dealing with them."

"Captain Pensky," Norlin insisted. "They're friendly. They're ours. Let's parley, and see if we can't—"

"No!" the genhanced officer roared. He danced around in front of the command chair, thin arms waving wildly.

"They're all against me. Since I left Earth, everyone's been against me. I suspect Droon of being an alien in disguise. A clever disguise, yes, but a disguise. Yes, that's it."

Norlin glanced at Miza and Sarov. Their expressions were unreadable, but for the first time he thought he saw real fear in Sarov's brown eyes. The tactical officer enjoyed combat; he had no stomach for fighting his friends and allies.

"We'll never surrender," Pensky said in a normal voice. His mood had shifted quickly. "Accept this input, Tactical Officer."

He swung around, sat in the command chair and confidently punched in an evasion routine. Norlin tried to follow the salient points of the plan and failed.

Sarov began to chuckle. He worked at his own computer to implement the plan.

The *Preceptor* leaped along strangely changing vectors, acceleration throwing them from side to side and the hull beginning to creak in complaint. Norlin watched the progress of the pursuing ships. Two heavy cruisers fired missiles; the *Preceptor* dodged them easily without using precious ECM missiles. When the battleship began firing its immense lasartillery, the true genius of Pensky's course became apparent.

Each bolt missed by kilometers. At no time did Norlin have the feeling the *Preceptor* was in danger, yet he knew the ships on their tail had been ordered to destroy them without offering quarter.

Pavel Pensky had the spark of genius. But was he right about the destroyer? Norlin didn't think so.

"Captain," came Miza's worried voice, "I'm picking up considerable disturbance ahead."

"Range?"

"Almost a light-hour distant from the Doppler reading." She gave the coordinates in relation to their rapidly changing position.

"The Death Fleet!" blurted Norlin.

He studied the woman's readouts and matched them with spectral analyses of the radiation waves he had ordered in the Lyman system. The match was perfect.

The alien Death Fleet shifted into the Sutton system. Thousands of ships.

"I was right!" cried Pensky. "The bastards *are* waiting for us. We'll lead our fleet to glorious victory. Our pennants will fly high as we march into combat. Forward, and let any craven slacker be put to the sword!"

"Wait!" cried Norlin. "You can't attack the whole fleet. There are too many of them. Even one is more than the *Preceptor* can handle. We need repairs. We need—"

"We need courage from the crew," snapped Pensky. "I shall supply all the genius required for illustrious victory in the face of overwhelming odds."

He leaned back in the command chair and acted as if wind blew in his face. Norlin had the fleeting impression of an ancient sea captain on his bridge, the stinging salt spray from a water ocean driving against his skin.

"Dammit," came Tia Barse's aggrieved voice from the hatch. "You're doing it again. You cut off my 'link. Ask for any more power, and the whole rust bucket is going to pop."

She hesitated when she saw the expression on Norlin's face. Her colorless eyes worked around the room, from the now-confident captain to the frightened Miza and the increasingly nervous Mitri Sarov.

"What's got everyone spooked?"

Gowan Liottey pushed past her and ran to the command chair. He leaned forward, his long, thin fingers gripping the arm so tightly that his knuckles turned white with strain.

"Please, sir, turn back. That's the Death Fleet ahead of us. I just saw it on the command vidscreen."

"An inspiring sight, isn't it? Thousands of them, just a small armada of us."

"You can't count on the ships behind us," said Sarov. "They're trying to blow us out of space."

"What in hell's going on?" asked Barse, confused. "I heard the auto-loaders working. Did this brain-dead son of a bitch fire on the *Death Fleet*?"

Norlin hastily explained all that had occurred in the past few minutes. Barse burst out laughing.

"You're no good as a practical joker, Norlin." She sobered when she saw the others' frightened faces. "It's not a joke? He really did blow one of our own destroyers to hell and gone?"

"He claimed it had been taken over by aliens—he called Droon a traitor."

"Captain Droon is no traitor," spoke up Pensky. "He is a victim, as were those aboard the destroyer. They've been taken over by the aliens. Clever mind-controlling bastards.

"But we're smarter. *I'm* smarter. Emperor Arian will reward me highly for this victory, and I don't mean those gaudy jeweled medals he's so fond of. He'll give me an entire world to rule. I'll do a good job of ruling, too. I want to rule. I was *meant* to rule!"

"Is he ranting?" asked Barse.

"He showed remarkable skill in getting away from the cruisers and battleship assigned to destroy us."

"Base ordered them after us?" Barse shuddered when Norlin nodded.

"Get the forward lasartillery online. I can't get any response from the guns. You, Liottey, do something besides suck on your thumb. That's unbecoming to an officer of the emperor!"

"Captain, break off. Return to base. We need protection. There are thousands of them!"

"Then our victory will be all the sweeter. What good is it when you defeat a weakling opponent? Only when you triumph over a stronger one is there any honor in it."

"The radiation cannon is hooked into primary and secondary power circuits," Barse said in a low voice. "Both circuits have to be activated for it to work. The recharging cycle will drain us for several minutes if we use it, though. It damned near blacked us out permanently the last time."

The *Preceptor* hummed as missiles launched. Norlin shook his head, trying to clear the buzzing in his ears. Strain mounted too quickly for him to bear. Firing missiles at this range was ridiculous. The Death Fleet had shifted into the system almost a light-hour ahead. The missiles could never reach the enemy; their drive engines lacked the range by a huge margin.

"He might be mining this cubic of space," said Barse, seeing Norlin's confusion.

"We'll need all the firepower we can muster when we get closer to them," Norlin pointed out. "We're driving hard into the center of their fleet!"

"Let's get ready. I don't want to die without the fixtures being polished," said Barse. "And Neutron might want to eat again, too. I ought to feed the damned cat a tank of methane and see if it changes any before it comes out his rear. Yeah, that's what I want to do before I die."

"Tia," he said, his hand stopping her.

"Mutiny?" she mouthed. Her colorless eyes danced. She took a deep breath and then shook her head. Aloud, she said, "What difference does it make how we die? I'd rather do it with all tubes firing and the radiation cannon draining my power than to have our own ships finish us off. Makes me think I died for something worthwhile." She snorted at Norlin's expression. "What's wrong, Cap'n? Didn't think I could be ironic?"

She left to do what she could to keep the cruiser under maximum power.

Norlin nervously paced, not sure what he could do. The command visor still gave him a complete readout

of the ship's status. They had improved their battlewor-
thiness in the past few hours, but they could never take
on even a small alien craft.

They had faced a mere scoutship and been lucky to
escape. Against the main body of the Death Fleet they
had no chance at all.

"We're doing well. They're coming for us. They're falling into my trap," Pensky said from the command chair.
He worked on his console and cut off Sarov. The tactical officer complained and was ignored. Sarov glared at
Norlin, as if he were responsible for the captain's suicidal behavior.

"Do you intend to take on the entire alien fleet?"
Norlin asked.

"Only those we can kill. For the moment, though,
there is something more important to do." Pensky smiled,
and Norlin saw no craziness in his eyes.

"What?"

"More tea. I had a delightful time with the ship's engineer. I must get to know my observer, also, and what
better way than a properly served cup of green tea?"

Norlin looked past the captain to Miza and Sarov.
They were lost.

"Very well, Captain Pensky. It would be my honor to
join you."

"Spoken like a true officer and gentleman. This way.
To the captain's quarters."

Pensky marched off as if he were in full dress parade
before the emperor himself. Norlin followed, gesturing to
the other two officers to return to post. Without a pilot
at the helm, there was now a chance they could change
the *Preceptor*'s course.

The table in the captain's quarters was already set
with fine porcelain cups. An autochef prepared the tea.

"It's not the same as having it done by a human, but
it will do. Primitive conditions on the frontier, you know.
You do know, don't you, Sub-Lieutenant?"

"Yes, sir, I suppose so. I was brought up on Sutton."

"Do tell me more."

Pensky gestured toward the chair opposite his. Norlin perched on the edge of the seat, rigidly at attention as if the academy commandant had summoned him. It was the only prior experience he'd had speaking with such a high-ranked commanding officer alone.

"What do you want to know, sir?"

"Your life, Sub-Lieutenant. How did you come to the academy?"

Norlin waited for Pensky to sip his tea before sampling his own. The bitter taste made his lips pucker slightly. He carefully replaced the cup on the saucer as he composed his thoughts.

"My parents were colonists from Earth."

"So, you are Earth stock? I thought so!"

"I hardly remember Earth. In fact, not at all. My father was a farmer and my mother a weather tech. Both were needed vocations on Sutton."

"Feed the masses and keep them happy with sunny weather," Pensky said. Norlin thought a hint of distaste entered the captain's tone, but he could not be sure.

"From as young as I can remember, I wanted to be an officer in the Empire Service. Education was hard to come by since my father was a farmer and it would be hard for me to break caste. My mother, though, got me a technical education. For several years I was in training to be a weather tech, but when I tested well, I got into the academy."

"Your parents? Still on Sutton?"

"Both dead, sir. My father died when a robot tiller malfunctioned. My mother, well, she never adjusted to being without him. They were the only family I had."

"No siblings? A pity. I grew up surrounded by hundreds of relatives. Emperor Arian is quite prolific, you know."

"I've heard," Norlin said. He tried to keep from grinning. From what the rumors said, Arian had sired more than a thousand children, all from artificial wombs. The emperor was too involved in the rule of the empire to spend time with a woman. Norlin had always imagined the man on the Crystal Throne with tubes attached to all his orifices, sucking and draining constantly.

"That's not too far wrong," Pensky said, startling Norlin by apparently reading his thoughts. "Arian seldom leaves the throne. It is a wearying life for him, but he has been gengineered for it."

"You're his third cousin?"

"Something like that. The imperial genealogists could tell you right away. Such family trees bore me. I enjoy being with people like Arian, whether they are relatives or not."

"Are you really...?"

"Telepathic? So I have been told," Pensky said, sampling his tea and peering over the rim at Norlin. "Does that bother you?"

"I had never thought it was possible."

"At the court of my cousin, anything is possible. We really are supermen, you know. Genhanced to the limits of human ability. My first cousin Leandra is immensely strong. She nearly crushed me to death the first time we..."

Norlin waited for Pensky to finish the sentence. Then he realized he did not want him to. Sexual relations between close relatives was illegal on the colony worlds but commonplace on Earth. Or so he had always heard.

"Lightning calculators. Physical abilities. My sister Peony combines both. She is a rarity."

"Your tactical ability is remarkable, sir," Norlin said. "Do you use telepathic powers to read the minds of your opponents?"

"Not at all. I have no telepathic power."

"But you said..." Norlin was confused now. He saw that this pleased Pensky. The genhanced officer was toying with him.

"It's a game I never tired of at court," Pensky explained. "We would try to confound one another. Only the cleverest among us ever figured out the truth."

"I'm not all that clever, sir."

"No, Sub-Lieutenant, you are not. But you have interesting abilities to offset your rather low intelligence."

Norlin bristled but held his anger in check. "Is this more of your courtly word play, sir?"

"Just an observation. It has been good having tea with you, Sub-Lieutenant. I doubt we will do it again." Pensky rose. Norlin had the impression of a man about to vanish into higher dimensions. Pavel Pensky was as thin as a silk strand, with ungainly arms. From the way the rest of his uniform flapped around his body, he might have been emaciated.

"To the bridge. You may watch, if it pleases you."

"Those are my orders, sir," Norlin said, but he spoke to the captain's back. Pensky was already on his way back to the command chair.

Norlin ran to catch up. As he entered the bridge, he saw that Pensky had already made a quick circuit of Miza's and Sarov's stations and hopped up into the command chair, staring at the vidscreen. Without looking down, Pensky began working the controls in the arm of the chair.

Norlin watched the preparations made by the genhanced officer as they popped onto the vidscreen. After putting on the HUD, he got a better sense of the captain's reasoning and marveled at it. Pensky had a true talent for tactics but no common sense. Norlin worried he might even have crossed the thin dividing line between sanity and the parti-colored wonderland of his own genius.

"They're locked on," came Miza's warning.

Norlin did not have to see the summary off the com officer's console to know she meant the aliens, not the pursuing Empire Service sub-fleet. Once more the *Preceptor* was going into battle against the aliens. As before, Norlin had no feeling that they would emerge victorious, even with Pensky's obvious confidence in his own abilities.

"Let us lead our forces into battle glorious and admirable," said Pensky with true satisfaction. He worked furiously at the controls on his chair arm. Sarov moved toward the command chair to protest. Norlin waved him off. Their position was untenable. The only hope they had for survival measured longer than in minutes lay in Pensky's skeletal hands.

"Chikako, contact the other ships. Warn them of the Death Fleet. They might have missed the indicators we picked up. Send a lasercom back to Sutton II informing them of the situation." Norlin's pulse pounded as he issued the orders. Miza didn't have to obey him, but she did. Someone on the bridge had finally shown a spark of judgment, even if it wrote their obituaries.

Norlin pointed to the jury-rigged panel where they had rewired the radiation cannon. Sarov went to it and waited, hand resting on the toggle that would send the prodigious beam of radiation into the center of the Death Fleet. It might be a suicidal one-shot weapon but Norlin vowed to take a few of the mysterious aliens along with him if they had to die.

"Missiles away. Oh, yes, we strike at their vile black heart. War is the highest perfection of human knowledge." Pensky began cackling to himself and rubbing his hands together as if trying to wipe away dirt.

Norlin checked the displays and saw that the missile placement was precise and deadly. Forty-eight missiles launched. Six alien warships were destroyed or damaged. The tactic of accelerating through the middle of the alien fleet had taken their opponents by surprise. By the time they realized the *Preceptor* was not vectoring away, it was too late to commit.

Even in the vastness of space, the aliens could not fire at the surging, crazily spinning cruiser without endangering the tight cluster of their own ships.

"They're parting ahead to give one subfleet a shot at us," warned Norlin. The aliens were quick to adjust to the unexpected.

"All ES ships behind us have been destroyed," reported Miza. "I got the last microburst from the battleship. It didn't stand a chance against one of the alien's heavy planet-beams."

The *Preceptor* lurched as the aliens began finding ways around damaging their own ships. Missiles popped up in front. Pensky's genius for defensive techniques stood them in good stead. He chuckled to himself as he worked Sarov's station.

The tac officer stood to one side and watched, his face bright red with anger. His finger tapped repeatedly against the toggle that fired the radiation cannon. Norlin knew he had to keep him calm—using the captured alien weapon required precise timing. If they fired too soon, they wasted their single most potent weapon. If they waited too long, the *Preceptor* would be space debris.

"This is tiresome. They keep firing. Why don't they stop? It's time for tea. Does anyone wish to join me?"

Norlin stared in dismay as Captain Pensky jumped from the command chair and walked away.

"Sarov, get back to your station. Now!" Norlin shoved Pensky away and dived into the command chair. He tried to absorb all the information flooding in. Wearing the command visor had prepared him, but the suddenness of knowing his orders would be carried out caused him to hesitate for a few seconds.

The aliens concentrated their radiation cannon fire on the *Preceptor*. Explosions deep within the cruiser echoed in Norlin's ears as he let Sarov fire their missiles at will.

He checked with Miza, saw the opportunity appear and reached for the toggle for the radiation cannon. He crushed it with his hand.

The ship bucked hard, and inky blackness descended. The radiation cannon had once more sucked every last joule of energy from the *Preceptor*'s engines.

Chapter Thirteen

"We're dead," moaned Gowan Liottey. "We're all dead!" The emergency lights flickered and came on, giving everyone on the bridge a jaundiced appearance.

"No," said Miza, kneeling beside Pavel Pensky. "Only one of us." She pressed her fingers into the genhanced officer's throat and shook her head. "He's dead, and I don't know why. There's not a scratch on him that I see."

"What difference does it make?" asked Liottey. "He's the lucky one. He's already dead. We'll follow in seconds. I know it. We're in the middle of the entire Death Fleet!"

The words galvanized Norlin who had stood staring at the fallen captain. He adjusted the command visor and circled the control room, checking each console against his heads-up display summary. The important readouts matched. Lesser systems deviated markedly, but he did not need them to keep the *Preceptor* alive.

He took a deep breath and resumed his position in the command chair. He hadn't liked giving up command to Pensky. Now, he was likely to be the cruiser's last captain.

The readings from Miza's sensors told a sorry tale. They had driven squarely into the center of the alien war vessels. The enemy had responded quickly. When they'd fired their radiation cannon, it had left the *Preceptor* a drained husk, but oddly, they were still alive.

"Ships everywhere," Miza reported. "No direction outward not filled with them."

"Weapons systems down. The radiation cannon took everything out. I'm going to back-up on the missile launchers." Sarov worked with a desperation Norlin had never seen before.

"Don't bother with that. There's not much chance we'd get to launch missiles powerful enough to do any damage. The ships around us are heavy." He marveled at their sheer mass. They were the planet-beamers, heavily armored and protected to withstand ground-based weaponry. To believe they had a chance of doing more than scratching a hull with their missiles was a fantasy beyond his wildest imagining.

"They think we're dead. They're sending a scoutship to board us," reported Miza.

"Can you intercept their communication?"

"No, Captain. Can't find anything anywhere, though they're too well coordinated not to be in constant contact."

"Telepathy. That's the only explanation," whined Liottey. "They can speak mind-to-mind. How can we defeat an enemy that knows what we're thinking?"

Norlin turned and glared at the XO. Legally, Liottey was next in the chain of command. Not turning the cruiser over to him would be a criminal act; it would be an even greater act of folly.

"Gowan," he said softly, "give me a full report on all life support systems. Do a complete sweep of every command circuit. Let me know how to best use the RRUs."

"The RRUs, yes, we need to repair quickly. Yes, aye, Captain. Right away." Liottey left for his post amidships, muttering to himself.

"You handled him well," complimented Barse. "Now do some fancy work and tell me how to handle the engines. We're power-drained, and it's beyond me how to get this bucket of bolts running again."

"You'll find a way," he assured her. "You're the best damned engineer in the Empire Service."

"That works with Liottey," she said. "Not me. But don't stop. I like hearing it."

"Especially when it'll be the last thing she'll hear," said Miza. "The enemy ship is closing. What do we do?"

Norlin leaned back, his attention on Pensky's corpse. His mind raced.

"What else *can* we do? Prepare for boarding. We'll have to greet our guests."

"We're not equipped for it, Captain. All we have are a couple laserifles and pistols."

Norlin shrugged it off. They had at least *some* weapons. "We'll have to make do, won't we?"

He tried to formulate a plan he knew would work. His mind refused to come up with anything brilliant.

"Tracking the ship," came Sarov's anxious voice. "Should I take it out?"

"No. Let the fleet go past."

He hated the idea of letting the Death Fleet go unimpeded toward Sutton II, but there was only so much a single cruiser—especially one damaged beyond simple repair—could do. His duty lay in staying alive.

"They're putting out grapples," reported Miza. "There are robotic crews on their hull. They're sending over ERUs to examine the ship."

"Barse, Liottey, take laserifles to the airlock and blast them *after* they're inside."

"Captain, they're going to drill through the hull. They don't care if they spill our air."

"Why *should* they care? They think we're dead. They certainly aren't interested in taking prisoners."

"Why enter at all?"

"The radiation cannon up front. They want it back — or they might think we've developed one on our own. No planet has used it against them. Why should an insignificant ship in the middle of the Sutton II system pop up with it?"

"We took out five of their heavy craft," reported Sarov.

"Energy levels are coming back," said Barse. "We need a more efficient generating system to supply that cannon."

"Let's see if we can't get it off their ship." Norlin had high hopes of luring the alien scoutship close enough to board and engage the mysterious crew in personal combat. They had destroyed at least three human-colonized planets and not once had they revealed themselves. His curiosity about them soared — and hope died when he saw how cautious they were.

The scout hung back a few klicks, and the robot salvage crew landed on the *Preceptor*'s hull. They began drilling a way in just aft of the crudely mounted radiation cannon.

"We don't need this. Sarov, what chance do we have of getting the scout with one shot?"

"Not good. They might be in touch with the other ships."

"Miza?"

"Can't say, Captain. I'm not receiving any crosstalk from their fleet. It's as if the ships are programmed and following AI routines."

Norlin considered this. The Death Fleet might be totally automated. If so, they might face only robots. He shook off the notion. It didn't seem likely that a computer intelligence directed the fleet. If that were the case, why strip the planets as they did? Robots didn't need such a wide spectrum of resources — and he had seen foodstuffs being loaded into one automated looting factory.

"Can we get them off our hull?" He checked his display and saw that the strain from the boring equipment had mounted to the point of causing a breach. The laser drills would penetrate the *Preceptor*'s tough composite skin in seconds.

"Captain, we can blow the section," suggested Liottey. "There's nothing there but storage."

"Good idea. Do it," he said, coming to a quick decision. "Blow the damned robots back toward the scout."

The ship shuddered as Liottey jettisoned the entire storage module. The cruiser was no longer battleworthy, but it hadn't been before getting rid of the invading robotic snoops, either.

"There are no other major warships within easy range, Captain," reported Miza.

"Engineer? What speed can we make at current power levels?"

"Quarter," came Barse's immediate reply.

"Tactical Officer, open fire on the scout. Hit it with everything."

Norlin watched as Sarov expertly launched the proper mix of missiles. Ten fired, three struck. The resulting explosion far outstripped the killing power of the missiles.

"They self-destructed. Suicide circuit," said Sarov.

Norlin slumped. He had hoped for a chance to study the alien power plant. How did they recharge their radiation cannon so quickly? Or did they? Did they rely on sheer numbers rather than superior technology? To fight them successfully, he needed to know everything.

"Analyze debris," he ordered.

He didn't care who obeyed the command. His own attention was focused on a minimum-energy, maximum-speed orbit back to Sutton II.

The engines fired for several minutes. Norlin shut them down when he saw the power levels drop abruptly.

"Thanks, Cap'n," said Barse. "I don't want to go dry."

"This is for the best," he said. "We must look as if we're drifting out of control and dead in space."

He checked Miza's display and saw that the Death Fleet had gone on, ignoring them. The planetary defenses would give them a true challenge. A single cruiser, crippled and tumbling through space, could be ignored.

At least, he hoped they thought that way. If they didn't, he and everyone aboard was doomed.

Job done for the moment, Norlin climbed down from the command chair and went to Pensky's side. The genhanced officer's eyes had fogged over with death. He didn't appear any different from any other dead man. Death leveled all ability — and cured insanity.

"We can feed him into the ignition chamber," suggested Miza. "He'd finally be good for something that way."

Norlin decided against it.

"I want him stored in a vacuum coffin. Captain Droon might want to ship the body back to Earth. He *was* the emperor's cousin."

"Emperor Arian has thousands of cousins — all from a test tube."

Norlin shrugged off her cynicism. He had to attempt to return the body to Pensky's kin. They should know how he died. The Empire Service had centuries of tradition, but few were stronger than seeing to those who had died in battle.

He grunted as he heaved the dead weight across his shoulders and lifted. Liottey came onto the bridge and hurriedly backed away.

"Get a coffin ready," he ordered the executive officer.

"Sorry. They were in the section we jettisoned."

Norlin cursed. "Empty a food storage locker, then. I don't want him rotting and smelling up the ship. It'll be days before we can get back to Sutton II."

❈ ❈ ❈

He dropped Pensky onto a table in the galley and went below to check Barse's progress. He could have made the inspection with a single glance at his command visor displays but felt he needed more personal contact with the woman. She was the only one on the *Preceptor* he felt any affinity with.

Chikako Miza's bitterness sometimes overwhelmed him. Mitri Sarov was too aloof and intent on his job. And Gowan Liottey shared so little in common with anyone Norlin often wondered if the XO wasn't more alien than those in the Death Fleet.

He entered the engineering section and was greeted by Neutron. The black cat rubbed his head against Norlin's leg and peered up at him accusingly, as if every problem aboard was his personal fault.

"He hasn't been fed today, and you looked like an easy touch," said Barse.

"I am. Feed him. That's an order."

"Wouldn't you rather I get the engines back into condition?" Barse lounged against a pile of parts that had been stripped from a converter unit.

"Both. Feeding him won't take long."

"Shows what you know," she said, making a wry face. "Keeping that cat fed is a fulltime job. About the engines—I've got an idea. I plugged into Chikako's board and took a gander at our vector and location."

"And?"

"Give me a few days and complete use of the robot repair units, and I can get the ship back into fighting trim."

"How? We're not going to be able to dry dock when we get back. Not with the Death Fleet working on Sutton II."

"Let sector base take care of itself," she said. "Chikako located the ship Pensky killed. We're in good position to salvage what we need from it."

"I thought it was completely destroyed?"

"Usable parts, Cap'n," Barse said enticingly. "I can use them, the ship can use them. They're going to waste out there." She sobered and added, "We can also recover bodies and return them with Pensky."

"We can," he agreed.

He considered their predicament. The *Preceptor* lacked enough firepower to aid in the sector base's defense. If anything, they would be in the way. The Death Fleet would have the planet ringed by now and be working on destroying all life with their deadly radiation cannons.

If the *Preceptor* functioned at full capacity, as Barse promised, they could serve the purpose intended by the Empire Service. A warship waged war—and they knew the enemy.

"Two days?" he asked.

"Make it five. What's the hurry? And another three to refit and get powered up to max."

"We can use the time," he decided. "Get Miza on the 'link and tell her to lock on to the dead ship."

Barse smiled from ear to ear.

"I already did. I knew you were smarter than Pensky, Cap'n." She slapped him on the back and turned to her work.

Norlin leaned against the converter unit, shaking his head. He had much to learn about command.

Chapter Fourteen

Aren't you finished yet?" Norlin paced back and forth in the engineering section, hands clasped behind his back. Barse watched him as she petted the purring cat.

"The RRUs are hard at work," she said, "and have been for the past week. We're almost back at full strength, but I need to try a different solid-state switch on the radiation cannon. If I don't, we're going to drain ourselves down to our shorts every time we fire than alien monstrosity."

"It saved us a week ago," he reminded her, his mind on a dozen different things. "We're going to start radiating energy when we're back to max. The Death Fleet pulled back from Sutton and is starting a blockade. They destroyed four cargo ships that shifted into the system. The instant we move a muscle, they'll be on us…"

"Like flies on shit," Barse finished.

She tossed the black cat toward the corner of the room. Neutron yowled in protest as he spun around adroitly to get his feet under him for an easy landing. He turned and glared at her, green eyes filled with disdain at such undignified handling.

"It doesn't matter," Norlin told her. "Even if we get only one shot with it, we're going to contact base. They've held out for a full week. They need to know there's someone who can help behind enemy lines."

"*In* enemy lines is closer to truth," she said. Barse heaved a sigh. "Cap'n, let me tear into an alien power plant. I need to know what they use. We're going to cinder ourselves shooting that damned popgun of theirs if I don't."

"You saw what their scoutship did on approach to take us into tow. It suicided. They aren't going to let us dance in and rip apart their equipment so you can reverse-engineer it."

"Never hurts to ask." She smiled crookedly then added, "Just a joke," when she saw his reaction. "We're going to full power within the hour. You ready to start swatting flies?"

"I'll be sure Sarov is."

Norlin went to the control room and studied the readouts. Barse and the never-tiring robot repair units had worked wonders in the past week while they drifted through space. The *Preceptor* lacked a few minor systems because of Barse's parts pirating, but she had put to good use the equipment from the remains of two Empire Service ships found drifting dead in space.

Both had been struck by the aliens' radiation cannon, killing the crews but leaving the ships essentially intact. Norlin would have preferred having the ES vessels at his side in battle rather than as parts donors, but that option was closed. Pavel Pensky had been too clever by far in blowing apart the first destroyer.

For the hundredth time that week, he reran Pensky's battle plan and studied the finer points. The man's tactical sense was unsurpassed. Like too many of the genetically enhanced, though, he had slipped over into insanity with no one daring to help him.

"Load the launchers," he ordered Sarov. "Here's our preliminary plan. Choose what you need carefully. We won't get a second chance to do it right."

He punched in the salient points of his approach plan and let Sarov work out the details. The tac officer handled tactics; it was up to Norlin to decide strategy—what their goals were.

"That takes us through the rear echelon of the Death Fleet," said Sarov. "We can skirt them and not use any nukes."

"I need the static from EMP and confusion," said Norlin.

"We can always shift and spread the warning," suggested Gowan Liottey. The sandy-haired XO wiped beads of sweat off his upper lip. Norlin wished the man would either grow a mustache, which seemed unlikely and might look ludicrous, or stop rubbing his lip.

He irritated Norlin with all his nervous mannerisms, although, in truth, he had pulled his weight more since Pensky died. For that Norlin was grateful.

"We've told sector HQ," he pointed out now. "We don't need to go any further. They've contacted other colonies by now. The Death Fleet can't stop all message packet missiles."

"They might. Communication is still spotty," the XO said, his voice growing increasingly shrill. "You know the attrition rate on courier missiles in shift space."

"This is our assigned duty station," Norlin said coldly. "To do anything other than attempt to lift the blockade is treason—cowardice in the face of the enemy."

"They might not even have faces," whined Liottey.

"Makes staring them down harder," said Miza. "But what's the difference? For you, Liottey, it's impossible to even look in a mirror without flinching."

"Full power, Cap'n," came Barse's terse, tense voice. "Sure you want to bull in like this?"

For an answer, he activated the attack program he had worked on for the past four days. All the computer simulations and mock battles meant nothing now. If he had erred in any significant part, the *Preceptor* would be dust floating through the Sutton system.

"Missiles loaded. Auto-loading ready for second firings, too, Captain," came Sarov's measured, deep tones.

Norlin stared at the back of the man's bullet-shaped head. He had let his hair grow until he looked like a bristly hog.

"I've got pick-up on an approaching enemy ship. Big one. We're not going to dance away from him." Miza's displays showed an alien battleship changing course to intercept.

Norlin cursed. He had hoped to take on a smaller vessel. The few scouts they had encountered had proven a match for the *Preceptor*. Such a massive warship outgunned and out-everythinged a Nova Class cruiser.

"Too late to shift out," he said. "We fight. Barse, get the radiation cannon power feed ready. Sarov, fire at will."

The *Preceptor* shuddered as Sarov's computer locked onto the target and sent a flight of genius missiles at the intruder. The AI circuits sought the shortest path with the highest probability of detonation on target. A randomizing factor had been built into the missiles to prevent a pattern from developing during long exchanges to further confuse enemy countermeasures.

"One impact. Negligible damage," reported Sarov. "We got its attention, though. Pre-corona discharges on three turrets. He's hot—and he's mad!"

"Comlink established with base, Captain," cut in Miza.

Norlin blinked in surprise. "How did you manage that?"

She shrugged. "Luck. No skill involved. They might be letting us through to see what we've got to say to each other."

"Who's on the other end?"

Norlin's attention focused on the computer display representing relative positions of the *Preceptor* and the alien battleship. Being burdened with official orders would only complicate the situation.

"Admiral Bendo from an underground bunker. The station has been destroyed."

"Captain Droon?"

"Vapor," said Miza.

"Keep firing the missiles. Ready the radiation cannon for one quick shot. A microburst, not a full blast." Norlin sucked in air and let it out slowly. "Patch the admiral into my 'link."

The line officer's face appeared a few centimeters beyond Norlin's heads-up display. Voice meshed with picture in a few seconds.

"Captain Pensky?"

"Pensky died during an attack. Sub-Lieutenant Norlin in command of the *Preceptor* once more."

"Highly irregular. You were — never mind. Report."

Norlin transmitted a microburst of coded information. Even if the aliens intercepted the nanosecond spurt, it would do them little good. The encryption could be broken, given time. Decoding it a month from now gave the aliens no edge.

"Received and verified with cyclic redundancy check. I'll put in for a medal for Pensky. An Empire Star, the same as we gave Dukker. As for you and your crew, Norlin, land in a shuttle at these coordinates." A sharp hiss sounded in Norlin's ear. He frowned, wondering what had happened.

On his private circuit with Miza, she said, "Got the microburst a few seconds before he said he was going to send it. The second burst is a decoy."

"Record," Norlin ordered mechanically. He was too engrossed in thought.

Admiral Bendo had ordered them to the surface of Sutton II. They didn't belong there. They needed to be in space where the real battle could be fought. Prevent the Death Fleet from landing its world-devouring metallic factories, and Sutton II was spared the destruction wrought on Penum and Lyman. Keeping the planet from total destruction such as happened to Murgatroyd lay beyond Norlin's hope.

"Indications the battleship's main turrets are warming for attack," came Sarov's even, measured voice. "Missiles away, each aimed at a gun emplacement."

Norlin glanced at the progress from Sarov's weapons display. Enough explosive power had been unleashed to level half a good-sized continent. The first two missiles hit squarely and didn't even scratch the hull.

"Why do you want us to land, Admiral?"

"Don't question orders. You have the coordinates."

"True coords marked, trap ones discarded, Captain," said Miza. "It looks good and official to me."

"Fire the damned radiation cannon," he ordered. When Sarov hesitated, Norlin used his command chair override. His finger stabbed down and hit the button with a ferocity he had not thought he possessed.

The *Preceptor* screamed in agony as the alien weapon discharged. The lights dimmed but did not plunge the ship into total darkness.

"Good work," he complimented Barse.

The only reply he received was a string of profanity as the engineer worked to fix the new damage caused by firing the radiation cannon. Norlin grinned when he saw they had disabled the battleship. The massive craft had taken the deadly beam square on the bridge. What had been destroyed aboard the vessel, he didn't know.

It hardly mattered. The ship tried to limp away. The mistake gave Sarov the opening he needed. Flight after flight of missiles sought out vital parts of the space-borne fighting machine and chipped away tiny pieces. The behemoth was being brought down by gnat bites.

"Got it. One up the rear engine exhaust," crowed Sarov.

The shudder that passed through the ship brought a cheer to Norlin's lips. He quieted. Only he and Sarov saw the victory. A human cruiser had met and defeated the largest ship in the alien's fleet!

"I don't want to see anything but molten droplets on the vidscreen," he told Sarov.

"Hard to do, Captain. The lasartillery is best for this work, and we're down two mounts, one dorsal and the other ventral amidships."

"Turning the *Preceptor*." Norlin worked the cruiser around its axis to bring the remaining lasartillery batteries to bear. Barse cursed even more volubly when Sarov powered up the laser cannon and began working on the battleship parts.

Norlin felt drained. He had wanted the battleship as intact as possible to study their power plant. Pragmatism had won out. He doubted the ship's destruction had gone unnoticed by the aliens. Reducing it to metallic vapor gave a better chance for evasion. Possibly—just possibly—the battleship's rescue party might hesitate and run spectroscopic readings to verify the ship's demise.

Every second he bought now gave him a better chance at survival.

"Are we really going to shuttle down to Sutton, Captain?"

Gowan Liottey stood beside the command chair, one hand on the arm. Norlin resisted the urge to brush off the trembling hand with the chewed decorative nails. Before he replied, he ran a quick life support check and cursory examinations on the other systems under Liottey's control. The officer had been doing well—and the *Pre-*

ceptor had been lucky. Little repair work on those systems remained to be done.

"Would you disobey an order from an admiral?" Norlin asked.

"We'd have to abandon the cruiser."

"Dangerous," agreed Norlin. Liottey's problem lay in stark fear for his life. Norlin's reluctance to obey came from finally realizing he was a spaceman. He belonged on a ship, not stuck on a mudball buried under kilometers of rock and metal shielding. Mobility gave safety; the *Preceptor*'s offensive weapons gave a different kind of safety. The idea of being on-planet and having to shoot at only those ships choosing to show themselves over the horizon bothered him.

"We can't disobey a lawful order," said Liottey. "Unless we mutiny."

"What are you getting at?" Norlin turned in the chair and pushed back the command visor so he looked squarely into the XO's blue eyes.

"The other ships. Rumors." Liottey glanced at Miza, who ignored him. "Mutinies. Crews refusing to stay and be slaughtered like herd animals."

"We can run or we can fight. We saw how unlikely the Death Fleet was to give quarter. Is running the answer to stopping them?" demanded Norlin.

"The galaxy is vast. We can drift in front of them. There are planets they'll never reach. Can you imagine them striking Earth? Impossible!" Liottey's eyes glowed with manic intensity.

"Each captain is entitled to deal with mutiny in his own way. It might be a black mark on the mutineer's record for minor disturbances—or it might be as extreme as tossing the miscreant out the airlock. Which do you choose, Mr. Liottey?"

"We'll die if we stay!"

"No one lives forever. Not even the emperor." Norlin turned and made a quick inspection of the major systems.

Barse was working well to bring them back to full power. She cursed constantly, and occasional yowls from Neutron could be heard punctuating her opinions on the heredity and personal habits of all captains.

He was amazed. She never repeated herself.

"We're going into parking orbit around Sutton II," he announced. "I don't like abandoning the *Preceptor*, but disobeying Admiral Bendo's direct order is even more distasteful."

"He's got the reputation of being a sharp strategist," pointed out Sarov. "It's not as suicidal as it sounds."

"The parking orbit is clear. The ground batteries are sweeping the sky in just the right pattern to protect our approach," affirmed Miza.

Norlin heaved a sigh and punched in the proper sequence to power down his ship and launch the small shuttle for the planet's surface. They were needed below.

He had to obey.

But he hated giving up the safety of his ship. *His* ship.

Chapter Fifteen

K eep the robot repair units working," Norlin ordered. "We'll be back soon and will need the ship in perfect condition."

The words burned his tongue. He knew he lied, not only to the crew but to himself. They would never return. Even if the others again assumed their stations on the *Preceptor*, he wouldn't be in the command chair.

Sub-lieutenants did not command cruisers. He had been lucky, and circumstances had smiled on him. The best he might hope for was a promotion to full lieutenant. The worst he didn't care to dwell on. Pavel Pensky had died. Emperor Arian did not like hearing his favorites had perished, even in the line of duty. If a scapegoat was needed to assuage the emperor, Norlin knew where he'd be found. Sub-Lieutenants were expendable.

"They've swept the aliens away for us with ground-based lasartillery," marveled Sarov. "The Death Fleet has pulled back and is allowing near-planet orbits to go unchallenged."

"Good," said Norlin. The last thing he needed was a fight all the way to Sutton's surface.

He hurried to the pilot's couch in the small shuttle-craft and dropped into it. The automatic straps closed around him. He ran through the preflight checklist quickly and saw that his program from the *Preceptor*'s master computer had already been loaded. They would follow the course given them by the admiral until they touched down at the main base outside the capital.

"Barse, close the lock. Liottey, check the air system. Miza, Sarov, hang on. Here we go." He hesitated for a moment as Barse cycled shut the airlock door. Then he stabbed the launch button that sent them blasting from the cruiser's cargo bay.

The instant they hit space Norlin knew something was wrong. The readings were off.

"Too little mass aboard. What happened? Liottey?"

"Captain, she's still on the *Preceptor*."

"What?"

"Barse. She closed the airlock from shipside. She's still onboard!"

"Damnation." Norlin grabbed the throat microphone and pressed it into place. He swallowed once to clear the circuit, then barked, "Barse, what the hell do you think you're doing?"

"Cap'n, good to hear from you. Having a nice trip?"

"We're coming back. I'll flay you alive for this."

"Captain, wait. Enemy ship moving in. Small. Scout class, I'd guess."

Miza worked the small console on the bulkhead next to her couch with as much finesse as she did the larger one on the *Preceptor*.

"It might as well be a battleship," Norlin complained. "The shuttle hasn't got anything on it."

"It's got us on it," said Sarov. "Can we land and let Barse do whatever she wants on the cruiser? Let her die if she wants."

"We're a crew. We depend on each other."

"Go on down, Cap'n. Let Baldy enjoy hiding his head in the sand. Me and the cat will have the ship ready to shift when you get back. There won't be a single system aboard that's not tuned to max or better. Two hundred percent, and that's a promise."

"Tia—"

He cut off his plea for her to rejoin them; his command sensors had finally picked up the incoming alien ship. Miza had been right. It was small, hardly larger than the picket ship he had commanded, but it leaked power all over space, unlike the other alien craft. This diminutive ship packed a wallop.

"Suicide ship," said Sarov, peering over Miza's shoulder at the readout. "We don't want to tangle with it, and we'd better hope the ground batteries can take it out. We're not going to outrun or outfight it."

"Outmaneuver it?" suggested Miza.

"Cold day in hell," said Sarov. "We'd need a bundle of luck and a star to wish on."

Norlin jerked forward and erased the landing program he had given the shuttle's computer. He put the nav computer on warning status and the controls on manual. The shuttle spun crazily and bounced off the uppermost layer of atmosphere.

"What are you doing? Trying to kill us?" Liottey's voice was a shrill scream and was drowned out by the struggling heat exchangers on the small ship. Norlin bounced them off the thicker reaches of atmosphere again, threatening the integrity of the ship and causing the temperature to rise perilously.

"That ship is accelerating on us like a particle falling into a black hole. We're not going to get away." Sarov sounded fascinated by the prospect of dying in one-sided combat.

Everyone cried out when Norlin hit the atmosphere at a steeper angle. Heat exploded like a bomb inside the small cabin. The heat exchange units gave up and activated shutdown circuits to prevent further damage.

He put the shuttle into a tight spiral. Computer warnings flashed all over his board. Norlin ignored them. He had to. Only one readout mattered.

The alien ship's tracking equipment proved to be excellent—too damned good for his taste.

"We're leaving an infrared trail for it, Norlin!" shrieked Liottey.

"Let's see how good it really is," Norlin said.

He tightened the spiral. He had bounced off the atmosphere like a skipping stone on water to kill orbital speed. Now he strained the shuttle to the limits of its design. Molten gobbets of glue holding together the composite material came free from the leading edges of the stubby wings. The structural integrity vaporized.

"Here goes nothing."

Just as he thought the shuttle might break apart, he put the vessel into a shallow dive. The g-forces blacked out Sarov and Liottey. Miza moaned, and Norlin clung to consciousness with sheer stubbornness.

"Hot," he muttered. He tossed his head from side to side to get rid of burning sweat dripping into his eyes. Everything blurred in front of him except the single readout showing position of the approaching vessel.

The alien sneak ship had lost them in the electronic fuzz of composite gas and the huge cloud of ionized air surrounding them from the reckless re-entry. As it sought them, it strayed.

Lasartillery on the ground spat out reddish-purple lances of energy measured in hundreds of terawatts. The planet's atmosphere was reduced to plasma, stripped of electrons in picoseconds by the mighty laser beams. The tip of this fiery tongue of coherent radiation brushed along the side of the alien ship at the speed of light. Pieces of invader tumbled from the sky.

"There," gasped Norlin. "We can land now."

He fought the damaged shuttle down through a gathering veil of pain-racked blackness. It had lost its control surfaces; his shoulders ached from the tension of pounding the computer in an attempt to restore fly-by-wire. Only after he touched down and skidded four kilometers did he relax.

"Good work, pilot," came the cheery congratulations. "You're going to be paying for this wreck for the next five hundred years—and that's only if you get promoted. Otherwise, a sub-lieutenant's salary won't cover your equipment damages for a millennium or two."

"Where am I? How close?" He struggled to match his landing with the area given him by Admiral Bendo.

"Good enough for government work. You're a few klicks from the entrance to base."

Norlin turned to see how his passengers had fared. Miza stood on shaky legs and helped Liottey up. Sarov bemoaned his sorry fate at having fallen in with crazy pilots but seemed uninjured otherwise.

"Out. Everyone out," ordered Norlin.

"That's dangerous," said Sarov. "The hull is outgassing. One small whiff could kill a dinosaur. And none of us are dinosaurs."

"*We're* not extinct, through no fault of our pilot trying," Miza grumbled.

Norlin checked the exterior sensors and saw that Sarov was right. He applied enough thrust to move the shuttle along the runway slowly. He ignored the outraged cries from the controller and the rescue squad on its way to take them to the underground bunkers.

"Drop out as I taxi," he told the other three. "They'll pick you up in a few minutes and get you to safety." He watched the tiny vidscreen as it picked up the lasartillery's actinic bolt of pure energy racing into the heavens in pursuit of new elements of the Death Fleet.

"What are you going to do? You can't stay inside," said Liottey.

"Barse is still in the *Preceptor*. With the suicide ship gone, I can get her off."

"You sound like a genhanced," accused Miza. "There's no way you can pilot this back to orbit, rescue her and return."

"You can take bets on how well I'll do. Now get out. If you don't, you'll be going back to the *Preceptor* with me."

The three jumped out the opened side emergency airlock, hit the glasphalt runway and rolled. Norlin saw the hovertrucks racing toward them. He swung around, checked the fuel and decided he had enough — barely.

His main concern was the shuttle's structural integrity. The composite matrix had taken extreme heat, vibration and stress reaching the ground. A wing might buckle. A hull plate might give way at a critical moment. Anything might happen.

Norlin applied full power and stood the shuttle on its tail. He arrowed directly into the sky, an inertial guidance needle showing the way to the *Preceptor*. The shuttle computer almost failed to compensate when the ship hit maximum dynamic stress. The air couldn't get out of the way of the blunt nose and swept-back wings fast enough.

Then Norlin found himself in space once more. The atmosphere clung to the craft with thin, grasping tendrils, but the real gaseous blanket lay behind. He pulled the shuttle around and achieved low orbit. Eighty minutes later, he applied braking rockets, rose to a higher orbit and jockeyed for position to dock with the *Preceptor*.

"Cap'n, you've got vacuum for brains," came Tia Barse's voice over his earphones. "Why'd you come back?"

"I thought you wanted me to feed the cat."

"You're crazy," the engineer said.

"We're a crew, dammit. We stay together." He had no time to argue with her.

"You're drawing them to us. There's another of the suicide ships. Wow!" Barse whistled as a laser spitted the craft. "Good shooting. I'd love to check out the servo-mechanism on the ground lasartillery. They're tracking better than we ever did."

"Get the refueling bay ready," Norlin ordered, not caring how the ground-grippers fired. That they aimed accurately was good enough for him. "We don't have much time."

"Cap'n, they really nailed that one. It had come into orbit just behind us when they gutted it."

"Good, glad to hear it." Norlin chewed his tongue as he fought the computer and the shuttle's balky controls. The chances for another safe landing on the planet in this craft were two: slim and none.

"This suicide ship's got a radiation cannon aboard."

"We've already got one."

"Right, and we can't use it because the power plant won't handle recharging. Let's take a quick look at their power system. It's not too far."

"You're going to be the death of me—of both of us. *And* the cat," grumbled Norlin.

But the idea appealed to him. He felt cocky. He had evaded an alien ship intent on destroying him, had out-piloted it, had delivered most of his crew to safety on the planet below. He was Pier Norlin, pilot without equal. He could do anything.

He shook his head, wondering if he had a concussion and didn't know it. Barse's suicidal tendencies had infected him.

"We get into the shuttle, we go planet-side. That's all we're going to do."

"Cap'n, have a heart. There aren't any other ships from the Death Fleet around. The ground batteries are holding them off right now. And they've got some cute little satellites that lock onto the enemy and chase 'em down. Let's explore while we've got the chance. It might not come again."

Norlin cycled open the airlock. Barse stuck her head in. He heard her voice directly and over his comlink.

"Please?"

"Got an RRU? Get both robots and a camera probe. I want pix of everything we see on that ship, as well as every piece of equipment the robots can pry loose."

"You're going to make one hell of a captain one day, Cap'n. You're not so bad right now." Barse jumped into a couch, cat under her arm, and studied the readouts. "You're holding this piece of shit together with a prayer, aren't you?"

"Not much else left," he admitted. Already the new mission began to pall. Good sense returned as the euphoria of his escape faded.

"Don't back out on me now, Cap'n," she cautioned. "I don't want to walk over there. Not after all the good work I've done while you were gone. Amazing how easy it is to work when you're not being disturbed all the time."

"Just you and the cat?"

"You noticed he wasn't on the shuttle?"

"That was why I checked the mass. You wouldn't leave the damned cat behind, but he would stay with you."

"I'm touched."

"Only in the head—like me." Norlin applied gentle pressure to the throttle controls and ordered the computer to get him out of the *Preceptor*'s cargo bay. They slid easily from the cruiser, spun around their minor axis and jetted over to dock with the alien ship slowly overtaking them in orbit.

"Looks dead," he said after several minutes of study.

"The laser beam sliced away the control room. Dammit. I'd love to see how they manage their cannon."

"No sign of hostile activity," he said, keeping a close watch on his sensor readouts. "The crew must have died instantly."

"Damned fine shooting, if you ask me. Let's not stand around with our thumbs up our asses. I want to prowl."

The long, slender needle of a ship had been treated with a dull, radar-absorbent, cadmium-based material; bits flaked off as Norlin gently bounced his shuttle against the hull. Using grapples, he attached the shuttle to the sneak ship just aft of the hole blown through it by the ground lasartillery.

"Let me get into my suit. You, too, Cap'n. We're starting to lose pressure."

Norlin groaned as he saw the life support system readouts. Barse was right. The shuttle leaked atmosphere like a sieve. He scrambled to get into the thin, transparent pressure suit. By the time he succeeded in tumbling and rolling in the free-fall environment, Barse had begun cycling through the airlock. Her suit bulged at the shoulder where the cat clung. The animal's eyes were closed; it was sound asleep.

"Wait. Don't go in there alone!" he cried.

"I'll be back before you know it. Keep the jets burning. I saw signs of incoming. This one must have put out a distress call before they died. I've got the RRU and the probe. Get to monitoring them."

Norlin fumed but obeyed—arguing now only wast-ed precious time.

He glanced at the long-range sensors and went cold inside. What Barse had tossed off so easily was true. A dozen Death Fleet ships blasted toward them.

"Hurry. They'll be here in a half-hour, unless the ground batteries can get rid of them."

"Not this time. I think their entire fleet's coming in for the kill. There. Just cut through the bulkhead and into their engine compartment. Can't make blivits out of it. Confused tangle of pipes and wire and spit."

"Start the probe. Get the robot repair unit working to dismantle what it can. Have everything photographed."

"You're babbling, Cap'n. I know what I want and how to get it."

Norlin's mouth turned drier than any desert and half as tasty when he saw how little time they had before the leading element of the alien fleet flashed across their orbit. A warship could release hundreds of independently targeting missiles as it rushed past the cruiser. No amount of supporting fire from the ground could save them if that happened.

The aliens might even think it was worth the energy expenditure to use their radiation cannon. Norlin pictured himself frying inside the flimsy pressure suit and didn't like the idea.

"Got it set up for relay back to the *Preceptor*. We can get it all in encoded microbursts when the robots are finished. Damn, but I wish I could do it myself."

"Get back immediately. I'm picking up the first data from the RRU and have a few good pix."

"Copy it all. The admiral will want to see it," Barse said sarcastically. "Dammit, Cap'n, don't you understand? I'm doing this for us. The *Preceptor* can be the hottest ship in the Empire Service fleet if we steal what the aliens have packed into theirs."

"What do they look like? The aliens?" asked Norlin.

"Who cares? We've got their engines open to us!"

Norlin estimated times and decided they had outlived their luck.

"Back. Now. No argument or I leave you."

"Make a man a ship's captain and see what it gets you," grumbled Barse. "He turns pushy." She returned quickly, checked the sensor relays and swung into the couch beside him. "You're so anxious to see Sutton II, let's go see it."

Norlin applied full throttle to the shuttle, ripping off grapples he had forgotten to detach. It didn't matter. Getting back to base would require ten times the piloting of the first trip.

Pier Norlin amazed even himself by landing just seconds ahead of the first barrage from space.

Chapter Sixteen

T he sky is turning black. Look at it!" Barse pointed.
The cloud-dotted blue-green sky darkened, the "storm
cloud" caused by hundreds of the huge planet-beamers
in the Death Fleet.

"Here comes a hovertruck for us," said Norlin. He
wanted to break and run; only a sense of decorum held
him back. They'd get under the kilometers-thick protection of the planetary defense shield in less time if he
simply waited. Even so, nervous energy and the need to
do something made his feet move in the direction of the
approaching vehicle.

"Race you for it," Barse said, smiling crookedly. Her
strange colorless eyes turned back to the sky. She clutched
Neutron tightly to her body until he squealed in protest.
She ignored him. "There's the first barrage."

Norlin shuddered when he saw the rainbow discharge
in the atmosphere. Each touch of the deceptively beautiful ray brought death to everything organic.

Immediate replies from the heavy laser cannon batteries on the ground showed that Sutton II was not sur-
rendering easily to the attack.

"Sounds as if they've automated. Those lasartillery emplacements won't roll over and die just because an ionizing beam hits them. No humans to kill."

"The aliens'll switch to electronics-killing frequencies if they have to," said Norlin. "Their radiation cannon seems to be tunable, depending on what they need to destroy with it."

He found it impossible to watch for more than a few seconds. His attention darted from the shuttle to the approaching hovertruck then back to the aerial battle.

The sky darkened even more as the Death Fleet moved into lower orbits. Each ship swung past faster, and there were more of them. He nodded approval for the tactic. Any individual ship received considerable punishment, but the speed in the lower orbit took it out of range quickly while the planet-beamer following it maintained almost constant bombardment.

Share the damage, concentrate the destruction.

The truck screeched to a halt.

"You two want a ride home or are you staying for the main show?"

"How many ships overhead?" asked Norlin.

"Who knows? Who cares? It only takes one of them to kill you dead, dead, dead."

Barse climbed in and scooted over on the bench seat until she was pressed against the driver.

"You have such a great philosophy," she said. "Tell me more. Maybe we can start a philosophic movement."

Norlin got in wishing only to be away from the landing field. He remembered vividly how the aliens had destroyed the fields on Lyman IV and Penum. He shuddered in spite of the afternoon's heat. And Murgatroyd. The planet was now a lifeless asteroid blet spinning around an uncaring sun. In a few hundred million years higher life might reappear—if some radiation-resistant bacteria had survived.

"What do they want? They can trade for everything they're taking. Why risk dying just for a few days of unhindered looting?" Norlin realized he had spoken aloud.

"You're the captain. You tell me," said Barse, turning from her quiet conversation with the driver. "What caused the Mongol hordes to sweep through Asia and Europe? Why did the Visigoths enjoy conquering more than the decadent pleasures of the Roman Empire? Why did Empress Aphia order Torrik IV destroyed, not that it worked too well? A whim. Maybe they're indulging in an alien whim."

"It might be a scavenger hunt. Ever do that when you were a kid?" asked the driver.

He and Barse started swapping lies about their youth.

Norlin turned away and stared at the bright rainbows shimmering in the distance and creeping closer. He almost slammed through the glasteel windscreen when the driver braked suddenly.

"Out. Into that tunnel. There's only one way to go if you're looking for a place to keep from having your head exploded."

"You've got such a way with words, Joe," complimented Barse.

"See you after my duty shift," he promised.

He slammed his foot down, and the hovertruck leaped away in a cloud of dust the instant they climbed down from the cab.

Norlin and Barse hurried down the narrow metal-lined, downward-sloping tunnel. He fought down feelings of claustrophobia. Spacemen couldn't afford such fears, yet this was different. The sense of the weight of the ground above him grew until he wanted to scream. Then, just as he thought his imagination would bring down the entire world on his head, the tunnel opened into a well-lit area filled with elevators.

Standing in front of each elevator door were two armed guards. Norlin turned when he heard metal scraping across fabric. More guards on either side of the door behind had leveled laserifles.

"Sub-Lieutenant Pier Norlin and Lieutenant Tia Barse, reporting as ordered," he said.

"Identities check," came a distant voice. "Elevator four straight to the Old Man's office."

The guards left their post and escorted them to the proper elevator. Barse sniffed and said, "What a bunch of pretty flowers. Not a fighter in the bunch. Liottey would approve of their aftershave lotion."

The guard on Barse's right started to protest. The instant his attention focused on her rather than the laserifle he held, she moved.

She swung around, wrested away the rifle and kicked his feet from under him. She towered above him, the laserifle pointed at the other startled guard.

"As you were, Engineer," Norlin said irritably. To the guards he said, "There's no reason to keep the rifles on us. Either shoot or stay at port arms."

He took the laserifle from Barse and tossed it back to the fallen trooper.

"What can you expect? They haven't seen combat. They're all garrison soldiers."

The door opened, and Norlin pulled Barse in with him before the soldiers overcame their shock and got mad. The tiny elevator pressurized, giving him a fraction of a second to brace himself. Then the bottom fell out of the world.

"Some ride," gasped Barse. "Reminds me of the first time I was in free-fall. I even feel dropsick."

"Don't get sick in front of the admiral," he cautioned.

"Hell, Cap'n, I was thinking of waiting to be sick *on* the admiral. Be the most fun he's had in days." Barse crossed her thick arms to cradle the cat and smiled her crooked smile.

Norlin swallowed several times as the elevator continued to drop into the bowels of the planet. After what seemed to be hours, the cage began to slow. Its deceleration was gradual but still almost drove him to his knees. The door popped open, and he staggered out.

The admiral's aide looked up from a console and smiled.

"Don't worry. I've been up and down from the Pit a thousand times, and I still walk like I'm drunk when I get out."

"Knowing you, Martin, you probably are drunk."

"Still the same old Tia, I see. Go on in. Admiral Bendo is expecting you. Don't take too much time. They're beginning to open up with everything they've got, and he needs to concentrate on our defenses."

He turned back to his work, fingers flying on the keypad and causing figures to march double-time across the vidscreen.

"Do you know everyone in the base?" Norlin asked his engineer.

"Seems that way, doesn't it, Cap'n. I make friends easy. Actually, Martin testified for me at my first court-martial. A good guy."

"*First* court-martial?"

"You don't think I'd still be a lieutenant after all my experience, do you, unless I got busted?"

"How many times?" Norlin was joking.

"Twice. Made it all the way to commander the last time before that incident on Megalith V." Barse stroked the cat sleeping in her arms. "Let me tell you about that ruckus. I—"

She quieted as the door slid open and they were beckoned into the admiral's office by another aide-de-camp. All four walls were covered with vidscreen displays. Norlin glanced up; the ceiling held its own display. It took him several seconds to realize it showed a slowly changing sector of space above the planet.

"I'm old school. I prefer to check visually now and then rather than letting the computers tell me what's going on," the admiral explained. "The display encompasses a complete revolution every ten minutes."

The screen winked white, then came back to show stars.

"The Death Fleet has wiped out some of your sensors," said Barse. "That's why you have blank areas. Do you know what's going on in those sectors?"

"We know from what is entering and leaving—and there aren't too many yet," the senior officer said. He settled into a reclining chair and stared at the ceiling. "I'm too old for combat, but there're not many others left." He sat upright and spun around, staring directly at Norlin. "Why didn't you mutiny?"

"What?" The question took Norlin by surprise. "I'm a sworn officer in the Empire Service."

"So were the captains and crew of fourteen cruisers, two battleships and a few score smaller ships. They saw the Death Fleet approaching and they mutinied and ran. Why didn't you?"

"I knew what they had done to Penum, Lyman IV and Murgatroyd."

"You're from Murgatroyd, aren't you, Lieutenant?"

"Yes, sir." Barse was unusually quiet.

"Rebel planet. Maybe we need more rebels. The empire doesn't have the backbone to stand tall any longer. Emperor Arian is more interested in his pleasures on Earth than governing properly."

"Sir, that's approaching treason."

"So court-martial me." Bendo heaved a deep, gusty sigh then coughed. "It's nothing you haven't been thinking. The service is only as good as its principles. I checked your records, Norlin. Nothing outstanding, but you do have a commitment and sense of honor missing in most of our officers. You're less than half my age but you're old school, like me. Yes, old school." The admiral heaved another deep sigh.

"Thank you, sir."

"Don't. It's a curse. I ought to pull out, let those bastards take Sutton II while I shift back to Earth. They won't attack the center of our society. They're not strong enough."

"You're working well against them, sir."

"Not good enough, but we've taken out adequate numbers to know we can defeat them. The independently targeting pursuit mines work pretty well for us, but we don't have enough to make a difference, not against thousands of ships.

"I've gone over the data you sent from Lyman IV. They always attack through infiltration and from positions of strength and surprise because we can defeat them if we're prepared."

"And if half the ES doesn't turn and run," put in Barse.

Norlin started to quiet her. Admiral Bendo motioned him to silence.

"She's right. We could blow them out of the sky in an hour if we had their cohesion of purpose. We had the will once. It's moved out to the far frontier." He coughed again. "It might even be dead in what were once our colonies. No matter. We have to fight, not philosophize."

The room shook. Bendo wheeled his chair around and worked on a panel so vast the individual controls lacked identifying labels. He reached into his jacket pocket and pulled out a small hand controller. He pushed back and began using the controller on the panel.

"Each lasartillery battery is keyed into the hand unit," said Barse. "No one else can use it."

"What does the board control?" asked Norlin. "It looks like a fire control board, but it's so huge!"

"All the planetary defenses flow through here," the admiral said. "I've already programmed in the general strategy for our defense. I make the second to second adjustments myself rather than letting the computer do it. Makes me think I've got some reason for being here."

Norlin nodded. His professors at the Empire Service Academy had been split on the proper use of a battle computer. Some claimed the faster responses of an electronic device outweighed the predictability they displayed. Others insisted no computer could match the human mind for integrating thousands of data bits and acting nonlinearly. Falling into a pattern turned a battle into a slaughter—the winner being the side that discerned the other's regularity of behavior and capitalized on it.

"They orbited and tried to use their radiation cannon. The station sustained heavy damage but was sufficiently prepared. The core remained intact, and a few officers fought back."

"The rest mutinied?" asked Barse.

"I'm afraid so. It didn't matter. The Death Fleet destroyed the station within an hour. That small resistance gave us ample warning and time to prepare, using data they collected."

"What of my warning?" asked Norlin, startled that no one had heeded the messages he'd sent. He had risked his life and command—for what?

"My aide ignored it. I never saw it until after our sensors picked up the leading elements of their fleet," said Bendo. "By then, it was almost too late. They infiltrated a dozen or more sneak ships that wreaked havoc on our fleet. Most were destroyed in dock."

He ran a shaking hand over the sparse gray thatch on his head. Norlin fancied he could see through the parchment-thin hand. Bendo spoke with authority, but his body betrayed him in subtle ways. He coughed again; this time, Norlin listened and heard a death rattle.

"My aide led a small group of officers in an attempted coup," Bendo said without turning around. He used the computerized controller to play the vast panel like a conductor with a massive orchestra. Lights flashed on and off; somewhere halfway around the world lasartillery batteries fired and surface-to-space missiles launched.

"The one outside? I've known Martin for years."

"Not him. Another. He's dead, even if his rebels still are trying to take control. They want to sue the aliens for peace and work out a peaceful coexistence."

"But—"

"I know, Norlin. I've seen your pix. So have they."

"But the aliens give no quarter. They obliterated Murgatroyd!"

"We've been at peace too long. It's as pernicious as being at war too long. You get to enjoy it, think it's the only state there can be. One makes you soft, the other vicious. I'm not sure either is much good in perpetuating the species." Bendo made a wide sweep with the controller and lit half the panel red.

Norlin blinked as the vidscreens blinked white then returned to their displays. Most of the lasartillery onplanet had fired. Behind its fiery bolts went a barrage of missiles, some of which penetrated to the Death Fleet because of the efficacy of the laser assault.

"Vary the attack. Catch them off-base with one then follow with another. And still another." Bendo fired the lasers again. "Doesn't always work, though. They're good. They're vulnerable, but you have to probe hard to get to them."

Norlin listened with half an ear. He had strayed to a panel manned by four under-officers. They struggled at some task the purpose of which wasn't immediately obvious to him. Then he understood.

"You've mined an entire moon!"

"Not mined. Something better," said the admiral. "Watch this. We damaged ten percent of their ships with the first major assault. This will be even more interesting. They expect the next attack from on-planet. The outer moon has been completely mirrored."

"Fighting mirrors?" asked Barse. "How do you position and aim them fast enough?"

"We're using continuous wave lasers for this attack. Chemically fired, slow-burning duration, high-energy oxygen-iodine." Bendo pointed his controller over the shoulder of the middle officer at the board. Red lights flashed everywhere.

Norlin jerked around and stared at the ceiling. The laser beams blasted at the speed of light from batteries on-planet, found their mirrors on the outer moon and were reflected. To the Death Fleet, it must have seemed a new enemy had attacked from spaceside.

"That took another ten percent of them, the sneaking bastards," said Bendo. "But it's not the major assault. Gordon, are they turning to the new attack?"

"Half rotated their weapons outward, sir," came the immediate reply.

"Take them out."

A new barrage of particle beams from containment-chamber, measured-detonation nukes licked upward. The bombs exploded, the searing radiation contained by rock and force fields, then funneled outward. As the first wavefront left, a new bomb detonated. By the time the chamber was reduced to force-field-backed slag, eight devices had been fired, the last one sealing the tunnel-barrel.

The planet shook and quakes racked the buried headquarters.

"We've destroyed half their attacking fleet, Admiral. The ships beaming the planet are reforming. Computer analysis is working, working, working. Can't identify this new attack formation."

"What do you make of it, Norlin?" asked Bendo.

"This isn't a pattern for space bombardment. They're protecting the ships moving in to reinforce what's left of the initial force. They might try to duplicate the attack they used on Murgatroyd."

He heard Barse's teeth grinding together when he mentioned her home world.

"The back of their attack is broken," pointed out the admiral.

"They're going to invade," Norlin concluded, not thinking. "No," he said quickly, "that's absurd. They can't land without having reduced the planet to rubble."

"Your instincts are good. Don't try to correct yourself. They're forming a shield to protect landing craft."

Try as they might, the ground defenses could not penetrate the tight shielding of ships around the huge cargo vessels in the center of the Death Fleet. Norlin watched in helpless fascination as the sky rained thousands of alien war machines.

They had been defeated in space. So, the aliens intended to triumph on the planet's surface, where the ferocious space-aimed lasartillery and missiles couldn't be used.

Chapter Seventeen

Stop them. Now!" bellowed Admiral Bendo. He used his controller to activate half a world of lasartillery. The fierce anti-ship beams found too few of the falling invaders.

"We can't track them once they land, Admiral," came the distressing report. "They're blocking our fine-sighting radars. Most of them will land at a point fifteen klicks southwest of the Pit's main entrance."

"They can set up mining operations there and drill through until they get into the southern corridors," Bendo said, after a moment's thought. "That's the shallowest point in the base. How'd they know that?"

"Who sold us out, you mean," said Barse.

She looked at Norlin. He had the same thought running through his mind. Mutiny and treason were cousins. Even worse, the aliens might have captured some of the ships trying to flee and interrogated the crews. He had been told at the academy of drugs that made anyone babble endlessly. The only defenses against them were ignorance and death.

If the aliens were telepathic, they might not even need drugs to interrogate their prisoners. And he doubted the aliens cared much if their prisoners died during questioning—that might even be desired.

Bendo swung around in his chair and preempted the base's main computer. Norlin blinked when he saw how powerful the computer was and how much of its capacity Bendo's tactical problem took. Several minutes later, the admiral released the machine for other uses.

He had aged a dozen years in the span of those minutes of computing.

"It's not good. We can shut off the section, but it's like cutting off our noses to spite our faces. Those are mostly storage rooms."

"We can live off..." Barse's voice trailed off when she understood the aliens' strategy.

"It's a war of attrition now," said Norlin, coming to the same conclusion his engineer had. "They cut off our supplies and wait for us to starve. They're in no hurry."

"We need a fleet to bombard them from space," said Bendo. "Without it, we're helpless to strike decisively. We've got almost no army to fight on the surface."

"The fleet's run off with its tail between its legs," said Barse. "So, turn the lasartillery on the spot. You can use the fighting mirrors on the moon."

"It's not that simple," said Norlin, understanding how the Pit's designers protected it. No one wanted the planetary weapons turned against the home base. The fighting mirrors would never—quite—be in position for a direct hit on the buried base. "What provisions were made for ground defense?"

"Not much," admitted the admiral. "Space-born invasion is impossible. Emperor Arian's best genhanced strategists agree on that point."

"Too bad they're not here to check their theories against reality," said Barse, a sour expression on her face. "We're not going to sit here and let them starve us to death. Give me a laserifle, and I'll hunt them down like the pigs they are."

Her fervor brought a short laugh to Bendo's lips.

"We'd have them by the short hairs if we had a thousand more like you, Lieutenant. There are a few CAVs in a position to do us any good. Transporting them from the rest of the planet leaves the remainder of the world vulnerable."

Norlin tried to remember what he had heard about planet-based military operations. A Complete Attack Vehicle carried cyclic-fire laser cannon, some small nuke capability and enough lanxide armor to withstand anything short of direct nuke hits and the lasartillery used by the base for its defense. He couldn't remember much else about its performance characteristics. He had focused on space systems, not ground-grippers' war toys.

"Check out the specs, Cap'n," said Barse.

Bendo had brought up the efficiency data for the CAV at the engineer's request. Norlin looked over Barse's shoulder.

"It doesn't look much different from the cruiser controls."

"They were designed by the same research team. The controls are similar, and the computers are identical in many systems. The life support is different, but not by much. The armament is lighter, and the variety of missiles is limited."

"How many CAVs do you have, and how many crews are trained to use them?" asked Norlin.

"Fifty vehicles, half that many officers able to roll them out and into battle."

"Let me try, Admiral," said Norlin. "It looks enough like the *Preceptor* for me to give the aliens hell, at least for a while."

"I think we can keep their fleet at bay now that they've landed ground forces. They'll let the surface fight rage on and possibly divert us. We don't know what they've brought down. This is a new stage of the conflict for us."

"This is a snap to run, Cap'n," Barse assured him. "You can do it with your eyes closed. Let's go burn a few aliens, and then I can get back to my ship."

Norlin's light-purple eyes locked on the admiral's.

"It will be *my* ship if we get through this?"

"The *Preceptor*? Why not? You're a better commander than half my fleet captains."

"Which half? The ones remaining or the ones that ran off?" Barse thrust out her chin truculently.

The admiral laughed harshly.

"The ones who matter, Lieutenant," he said.

"It's a damned shame a lowly sub-lieutenant has to command a line vessel," continued Barse. "He ought to be at least as exalted as any of his crew."

Bendo scowled then tapped a button and studied the vidscreen for a moment.

"All right, Commander Norlin. Get your crew into a CAV and blow the hell out of them. Then you can get back to your cruiser after you've won this battle for us."

"That's the way we operate, Admiral," said Barse. "We can do two impossible things before breakfast and kick ass all the way to lunch."

"What's the battle plan, Admiral?" Norlin's head spun. He felt as giddy as he had when he'd found himself so unexpectedly in command of the Lyman IV station.

"Get the CAV out of storage, find the enemy, destroy."

"That's it?" Barse snorted and shook her head. "Get the others down here; we'll put together a real plan. How much different can this be for Sarov? CAVs instead of cruisers. Two dimensions instead of three. He can do it standing on his head. He's the tactical officer."

Norlin barely noticed Bendo nod in agreement. He drifted toward a computer and began putting his own problems into its electronic maw.

Tapping into the full battle knowledge of the base helped; remembering the way Pavel Pensky approached tactical problems aided him even more. The genhanced officer had been more insane than not, but his flashes of genius had given Norlin tremendous insight into outrageous tactics that worked against the aliens.

The layout of the Pit bothered him. Getting to the alien landing force would be easy. However, if they penetrated into the storage area, they could race along, drill back to the surface and cut off any hope of retreat.

"We can't match them in the tunnels if they break through. They'll have armor and superior support. Admiral, how many soldiers can be stationed there?"

"Five hundred. No more. All they have are sidearms and laserifles. There aren't any heavier weapons inside the Pit."

Again Norlin saw the influence of genhanced planners. The underground base need not repel invaders. That meant they had no reason to require heavier equipment.

"We have to stop them from penetrating. Once they do, they can flood the Pit with poison gas, water, anything they can bring down from the surface. They don't want to occupy this post; they want to destroy it and everyone in it. How much armored shielding is there above those rooms?"

The admiral shook his head.

"I can't find those blueprints. We've sustained some computer damage from quakes. The best anyone recalls is a klick of solid rock and as much as three meters of lanxide laminate."

The rock might melt away in seconds with the proper laser drilling equipment. The lanxide ceramic neither cracked nor melted easily. The aliens would have to sublimate it, and Norlin wasn't sure if that could be done with portable laser drills.

"They'll blast," he said suddenly. "They'll nuke the area then return and come inside."

"That's dangerous for them," said Barse. She turned as Miza and Sarov entered. "Where's Liottey?"

"He's trying to get reassigned to something less dangerous," said Sarov.

"He wants to be a sanitation engineer and spend his hours watching shit flushed through the pipes," Miza added. "He'd be great at it. All he has to do is match up what's in his head."

"There he is," said Norlin. "Look this over. Tell me what you think."

He brought his crew into a tight circle at the console and began working out his battle plan. Sarov made revisions, which Norlin accepted. Miza scoffed at it all; he ignored her. Barse gave a list of material needed. He passed this along to the admiral. Gowan Liottey almost wept as he pleaded to be let out of the mission.

Norlin considered having the man shot. Only the need for a decontamination officer on the CAV deterred him.

"I've got the program ready." He pulled the ceramic memory bar from the computer and tossed it to the admiral. "Have this programmed into the other CAVs. We'll need as much coordination as possible with the initial attack. Then it's going to get messy and no plan is likely to succeed. We just shoot at anything moving that doesn't look like another CAV."

"You're in charge, Commander. Good luck."

Bendo thrust out his frail hand. Norlin hesitated, unsure of himself. Then he shook it. The admiral's grip was surprisingly strong.

He stepped back and saluted. Curious feelings of exhilaration and dread mixed in him. He was in command of Empire Service ground forces entering a major battle. Responsibility weighed heavily on him, but a more elemental worry turned him hollow inside.

He would never survive this battle. Fifty poorly piloted CAVs against an unknown alien force was a suicide mission.

"Forty-two CAVs are assembled on level three," said the admiral. "Get into the field as quickly as you can, Commander."

The three crew members who didn't know about his promotion earlier looked startled. Sarov and Miza accepted it. Liottey tried to protest. Barse shut him up with an elbow to the ribs.

"Come along, Gowan," she said as he gasped for breath. "I'll show you what you have to do. And heaven help you if you make even a teensy mistake."

Norlin checked a last time to be certain the other CAV battle computers carried his attack plan. Only forty-two functional, manned vehicles. This mission had become increasingly suicidal and less likely to succeed.

He would die trying to repel the aliens. His death might stop them from raping and plundering other human worlds.

He walked onto the glasphalt staging area where the CAVs huddled like huge ceramic bugs. The hull design and composition turned away radiated energy throughout the spectrum and protected against acids, poison gases and many types of shaped-charge projectiles. The stubby laser snout showed four cylinders; once rotating, each shared a quarter of the prodigious total energy output. Small lumps hid the mag-rail missile launchers.

"No nukes," reported Sarov. "I checked. They never allowed any storage within the Pit."

"We're going out naked, then," Norlin said. "That doesn't change the battle plan. Let's see what the interior is like."

"Yeah, we should be able to pick our own coffin," Miza commented.

Norlin dropped through the hatch and crawled forward. The cockpit proved more spacious than he had anticipated. The computer controls were a simpler version of his command chair on the *Preceptor*. He donned the heads-up display helmet and looked around. The HUD gave a full exterior view while showing small summaries of their weapons systems. Tilting his head in different directions brought up sensor readouts and target coordinates.

"Everyone at their stations?" he ordered, using the throat mike. He adjusted the tiny button earphones and settled into the overstuffed couch, letting its arms reach up and cradle him. Using the HUD, he controlled the entire CAV.

Acknowledgments flashed across his display, and he switched to the inter-vehicle comlink to get the small defense force moving. He held on to his nerves. Curiously, even though he knew he would never return from the battle, he wanted to get started.

The force rolled up three levels onto the glasphalt runway he had used to land the shuttle. The staunch ship had been reduced to a molten puddle during an alien ray bombardment. Norlin swallowed hard and sent a crackle of static over his throat mike when he saw a hover-truck with the front section blown off.

He hesitated about commenting on it. Then, Barse said, "That's one date I won't have to keep. Hell of a way to keep from seeing me, though. Joe could have been one of the good ones."

Her cynicism settled his nerves, letting him concentrate on learning the layout as the CAV whined toward the kilometers' distant site where the aliens fought to establish their beachhead.

He had less than a minute to study the CAV before Sarov shouted, "Incoming!"

The vehicle lurched as a countermeasures missile blasted from its tube.

"Destroyed," confirmed Miza. "Proper radio static burst of primary and secondary detonations received."

"Any chance of a retaliatory barrage against their launchers?" he asked Sarov.

"We don't have enough firepower for that, Captain. Or is it Commander?"

"Captain is fine. This hunk of junk isn't the *Preceptor*, but it's close enough and I'm still in charge."

"It leaks," complained Liottey. "We'll never withstand a gas attack. I know they'll try to gas us."

"Secure the damned seals," snapped Barse. "Do your job, and we'll all live to brag about this."

Norlin ignored them. He studied the advance of the other CAVs. Two had been disabled when they neglected to counter alien missiles. Forty against untold numbers with incalculable strength and capability. He needed more information.

"Miza, can you patch through to the *Preceptor*? Comlink and tap into the ship's sensors. See if you can't get a picture of the ground and the alien troop placement." He had to keep telling himself this was the same as space warfare, except for the dimensional limitation.

Norlin swore because he had neglected to get the recon earlier. The pix from the *Preceptor* relay showed him the gross features, but nothing in the detail he wanted.

"Sorry, Captain," said Miza, anticipating his next request. "All the survey satellites have been destroyed. The Death Fleet scouts are good at what they do."

"We know enough to get started." He tapped in instructions that were microbursted to the other CAVs over continuously changing frequencies. Even with their broad communications spectrum static the aliens couldn't block all the orders.

The CAVs rolled into attack formation. Norlin's fingers twitched in anticipation as he paused above the button that would issue the command.

He stabbed his finger down decisively. Forty cyclic laser cannon began firing simultaneously as the vehicles advanced into hell.

Chapter Eighteen

They never saw where the missiles came from. One instant Norlin was shouting for them to charge and firing the heavy cycle lasers on the CAVs' turret. The next instant the ground turned to jelly under the heavy tracks.

The sudden disorientation as the barrage melted the rock under the CAV and hammered it with one shock wave after another caught Norlin by surprise. His space training enabled him to recover quickly.

"Just like orbiting over an unexpected masscon, isn't it, Cap'n?" called Barse. "We got problems, though. The right track is jammed. A bit of molten rock oozed in then hardened."

"Work on it. What about air supply? I taste something bitter, metallic."

"Burning metal odor from outside," reported Liottey. "I can't seem to filter it. The entire vehicle is a sieve, I tell you. We have to turn back."

"Shut up, Liottey, and do your job. The filters have to work better than this. If not, I'll use your skin for a filter. Sarov, what can we do to make life miserable for them?"

"We're doing it. The other CAVs penetrated nicely. We're the only one sitting in the middle of a molten lake. Permission to use the laser as an anti-missile defense."

"Do it." Norlin craned his neck to get as complete a look at the readouts as possible in his HUD before trying to get them moving.

He strained forward and watched the exterior terrain turn to putty and flow downward viscously.

It took several seconds for him to realize the sensors were filtering the brilliant flashes as incoming missiles continued to detonate directly overhead. In space he seldom asked for a direct visual because the distances were so great and the computer kept adequate data flowing to him. Somehow, being on the ground, he felt the need to see everything.

He looked up and saw dozens of starburst patterns spreading across the sky. Sarov effectively shot down the deadly torrent, but the heat generated by the detonations formed a bubble over the CAV hot enough to cause exposed rock to burn and fuse.

"We can't stay here long. No wonder the air filters are failing." Norlin glanced at an exterior thermocouple reading and saw it registered well over 1600 degrees—enough to melt iron.

"Track cleared. I lost a few gears to do it, but you can run us up the side of a mountain now," reported Barse.

Norlin engaged the gears and had the computer search for the best path out of the smoking pit that threatened to swallow them whole. The CAV found solid ground, shook like a wet dog and growled. After these almost-organic maneuvers, it shot forward, leaving behind the downpour of missiles.

"Any nukes used?" he asked Miza.

"None I've found. We don't have any, and they're not using them. No good reason, as far as I can see. They can wipe us all out with a few well-placed megatons."

Norlin roared to the top of a small rise. From this vantage point, he got a clear view of the battlefield. His force had been decimated in the advance. Four CAVs were burned-out hulks, their crews dead long before the vehicle around them quit working. Ten others were damaged to the point of immobility. Norlin got them firing in directions to maximize their potential. He and the crews inside those damaged CAVs knew they were easy prey and wouldn't last long unless the aliens were kept busy by the fighting machines still operational.

Norlin worked quickly to add new details to his overall plan. Miza microbursted the orders as he magnified his view of the alien battle tanks.

"They're giant black metal beetles," he heard Liottey say. "Just like the ones on Penum the scout pilot saw."

"Got any insecticide aboard?" asked Norlin. "We can use it on them."

"The poison gas tanks are only half-full," replied Liottey.

"We have some? What kind?"

"Type K persistent. Instantly fatal to all oxygen breathers, works on filter elements and clogs them, has some acid content for pitting metal."

"Canisters or rockets?"

"Small rockets."

"Sarov, launch them immediately. I want a cloud sprayed across the valley where the aliens have established their beachhead. We have to keep them from drilling into the base."

"Done. Liottey, help me for a minute."

Norlin waited impatiently for the rockets to soar into the air then arch down into the valley. The alien lasers picked off the rockets easily. As they snuffed out each one, however, it created a heavier-than-air cloud of deadly oily fumes that descended slowly.

"Damage report," he ordered.

"Not too good, Captain," said Miza. "They might have been taken by surprise, but it didn't hurt them. There wasn't even much increase in com between units."

"I wish we could listen in and understand what they're saying. The computer doesn't give me any idea what their most likely response will be."

He continued to feed information into the tiny tactical computer and rearrange his attack to deliver maximum damage to the enemy. As more units failed or were destroyed, his tactics changed. He worked to preserve the remaining CAVs, even if at the expense of lesser damage meted out to the enemy.

"We're getting company, Captain," said Miza. "Two of the beetles are moving in the valley. Swinging around. Picking up sensor radiation. They're locking on to us."

Norlin's HUD flashed red to signal impending attack an instant after her warning. He let the CAV main computer evade—he wanted to concentrate on the enemy's mode of assault.

They didn't attempt anything tricky. Both fighting machines came directly upslope, their small but deadly radiation cannons firing as they came.

He ordered the CAV to remain partially shielded by the hill to minimize damage. Although the vehicle carried shielding adequate for the crew to endure a distant nuclear explosion, such concentrated radiation would ionize them within a few minutes.

"Tia, run full analysis on the tanks. Figure out how they're able to recharge so fast and keep firing with a mobile unit."

"This hunk of tin doesn't have equipment like that, Cap'n. I'm lucky to be able to run a tiny RRU outside—it's only got four robots and they're primitive. Let's finish off the buggers and get back to the *Preceptor* where we belong."

He heard the others mumble their agreement. He worked even harder to make that wish come true. His fingers flew over the computer keys, seeking weakness in the alien battle plan. He didn't find it. If the aliens maintained position in orbit, they could beam the surface and protect their base indefinitely.

"Get the admiral. Find out the status of the Death Fleet. We might need heavy lasartillery ground support to keep them occupied in orbit while we get rid of the vermin here."

"No need, Captain. The Death Fleet is withdrawing. Only a few dozen support vessels are still orbiting."

"They're breaking off the battle?"

"They're leaving. Reports are coming in from our scouts throughout the system that the fleet is shifting out. The admiral counts this as a victory."

"It's not," said Norlin. "Tell him they think they can maintain this base and keep pressure on us without the fleet." He worked over the facts and tried to see them as the aliens might. He didn't like his conclusions.

The enemy saw the power of the Sutton on-planet batteries. They had lost ships in orbit but managed to land a significant ground force. The planet's space power had been crushed. The aliens thought they had nothing to fear from above. Sit, drill, take the storage rooms, expand their presence gradually throughout the Pit—and win.

"We've got to stop them before they burrow down into the Pit," he said. "They're sure they can win and don't need to take further casualties in their space fleet."

"Cutting their losses here and running?" asked Sarov.

"They're *taking* their losses, not running. They think they're going to win Sutton," Norlin corrected.

"Crazy way to win. You don't pull out your strongest chance of winning unless..." Sarov's voice trailed off as he realized what the aliens thought of the CAV attack.

"We've got to convince them they're wrong, that we are a significant danger to them," Norlin added.

"Here's our chance, Captain. Beetle directly ahead!"

Norlin heeded Miza's warning and took control away from the CAV's computer. He swung around, protecting the side with the damaged track and taking a string of kinetic bullets against the armored turret. The aliens were trying to disable the laser cannon but not destroy the CAV.

"They want us for specimens," he told his crew. "They aren't going to destroy the vehicle, they're going to disable it and take us to their labs."

He knew such an emotional appeal would have little effect in other circumstances. Miza's cynicism surrounded her like an impenetrable shield. Liottey was too frightened to care. Barse simply did her job and needed no pumping up. Sarov fought for the cool, logical pleasure of it. This time, it worked.

They pulled together with fire and determination. Their laser cannon swung on-target, and a full thirty seconds of beam splashed against the first metallic beetle. Just as a red glow started on the side, Sarov fired the missiles. Each one found the hot spot and burrowed a little deeper.

It was Miza who suggested they ram. Norlin turned the CAV around and shot up the incline at full speed. The front of the CAV crashed into the alien tank with enough power to lift it into the air. For a second, both machines hung suspended belly-to-belly. Sarov fired another missile and broke the stalemate imposed by gravity. The CAV twisted around and crashed onto its tracks. The alien tank landed on its turret and slid down the hill, unable to right itself or stop its downward plunge.

Halfway to the bottom, another CAV used its lasers to rip open the alien's exposed belly. The rush of hot gases from the inside announced the alien crew's death.

"Organic molecules released," came Miza's report. "They're soiled, oiled and boiled."

A cheer went up. Norlin paid no attention. The second enemy beetle had circled the hill and now attacked from the side. The alien's radiation weapon threatened to cook them alive inside the CAV.

He jerked the vehicle from side to side, but the enemy followed relentlessly.

"Get him off us. Disable his cannon," he shouted.

Sarov tried. The lasers hit with deadly accuracy. Missiles crashed into the side of the other tank. A small rocket laden with poison gas veiled the metallic beetle.

Nothing stopped it. The machine kept coming, the deadly radiation weapon firing.

"We're losing control, Cap'n. The radiation is taking out my solid state controllers. Even the radiation-protected GaAs picochips. I don't want to think what's going on inside me."

Norlin knew the frightening answer to that from the danger warnings on his gamma counters. Their corpses would glow blue for a thousand years if he didn't stop the other tank.

He forgot about the battle raging to stop the alien drilling operation and concentrated on saving his own life.

The hillside provided a moment's respite, but the seismic pickups told the story. The alien tank was circling and would come directly at them in a few seconds.

"The tank's going to crest the hill. Hit it on the underbelly!"

Barely had he snapped out his command than the alien tank rose up as he had expected. At precisely that instant, Sarov hit it with a full laser blast.

The rotating laser tubes clanked and moaned as thermal expansion caused them to bang against their mounts. Each tube carried only a quarter of the full load; all were overheating.

"The lasers aren't working," Sarov said. "And I'm out of missiles. We're going to have to run."

"Track is acting up. We can't get full speed no matter what I do. I can't figure out what the hell's wrong, either. This isn't any fit way to travel, Cap'n."

Barse sounded more irritated than afraid. Norlin took strength from this. They weren't panicking. He wouldn't, either.

The alien beetle had been dented, and huge gouges were ripped from the exterior where the lasers had struggled against the tough metal. But the tank had taken the best the CAV offered and still came on.

Norlin couldn't outrun the alien, and he couldn't outfight it. All that remained was to die. He'd die fighting.

The radiation levels shot up to deadly levels as the alien opened with its cannon again.

Chapter Nineteen

P ier Norlin searched the heads-up display for some hint on how them might escape the alien tank. His fingers worked to tap in commands — that accomplished nothing. Radiation levels rose. He imagined himself cooking in his own skin. Sweat poured down his face and stung his eyes. In desperation, he returned the CAV to computer control and ordered total evasion.

He yelped when the nose of the CAV dipped and began to burrow into the ground. The laser cannon fired constantly to create the excavation. Indicators flared when one tube cracked and the lasing gas leaked from the chamber. He ignored it and watched in horror as the CAV dug its own grave.

"Radiation levels are dropping," came Miza's report. "We're in trouble but not danger. Good work, Captain."

He blinked the stinging perspiration from his eyes and realized the cynical Chikako Miza had complimented him on his quick thinking — when it had been due solely to the computer's AI programming.

"We're leveling out. Seismic detectors show the beetle above us. We're moving under it about five meters."

Norlin turned his HUD upward and saw nothing. Only dirt surrounded the CAV; they burrowed underground like a huge ceramic-plated mole. Then, the CAV lurched upward and burst into sunlight. Norlin thought they had launched into space; he looked directly up and saw only blue-green sky.

The CAV's partially disabled laser cannon fired at the rear of the enemy beetle. It had dived and surfaced to take the other tank by surprise.

The firepower remaining to the CAV wasn't up to the task of destroying the alien craft. Bits of metal erupted from the enemy's armor, but the beam failed to penetrate.

"We're in big trouble now," Norlin said. "We didn't get a clean kill."

"We didn't get shit!" cried Miza. "It's on to the diving maneuver now, too."

He tried to decide how best to die. Running was out of the question with one track malfunctioning. They could only keep fighting and hope for a miracle.

"Captain?"

"Don't bother me now, Liottey."

"There's a way to stop it. I want to try. Please."

Norlin adjusted his heads-up display to show his XO. The man was frightened but not as much as he had been earlier.

"What is it? And be quick."

"Firefighting foam. Look at their air intakes. We can stall it!"

"Spray!" ordered Norlin. They had nothing to lose and everything to gain.

The CAV exploded in a wash of foam as Liottey activated every external firefighting foam nozzle. The sticky white spray, intended to smother even nuclear fuel fires, caught on the wind and blew across to cover the aliens' tank.

"Laser cannon, stand down," ordered Norlin. He didn't want Sarov continuing to fire and vaporizing the foam. That would undo any possible advantage this ploy might enjoy.

Laboring to swing his vehicle around, he made the alien chase him. Their sensors followed him easily; infrared and radar were not blinded by the foam. Only visible light was—and, he hoped, their intake vents.

"What's going on, Cap'n? I'm watching that metal insect, and it stops sucking air. I'm getting heat readings that show a meltdown in their turbines or whatever they use. Nothing, not even our ceramics, can take that heat."

"Confirmed, Captain," said Miza.

"Good work, Liottey," he complimented. "Are they dead or just unable to move?"

"Engines are dead. Crew is alive. Comlink has turned active. Bet they're swearing a blue streak at their command center. I can almost hear them whining to be rescued!"

"Let's see if we can't eliminate that chance for them." Norlin turned the CAV toward the valley and saw fierce fighting along the slopes as the aliens tried to escape.

"Poison gas finally took them out. The acid content ruined their machinery. The aliens aren't too bright when it comes to filtration. I'll bet the poison gas sucked directly into their drills' air-coolant system. Not much is running, except the aliens."

Norlin drove downward, laser cannon firing fitfully. Sarov worked to his limit, and in conjunction with others in the force accounted for a half-dozen alien beetles. The CAV bounced and bobbed and once more bored through a small hill to emerge firing in the midst of an alien force. The difference between this and earlier fights was marked.

The aliens fled; the Empire Service attacked.

They attacked and won.

Norlin ordered a halt when the last alien tank had been destroyed. He conducted a quick check; only fourteen CAVs remained, none fully operational.

"You've done great," he said, both to his own crew and to the others over a general comlink. "Let's do some mopping up."

He microbursted new orders to the survivors. They prowled the area where the aliens had started drilling into the Pit, intent on finding booby-traps or pockets of resistance and neutralizing them. It took the better part of the day to complete this mission, but eventually only Empire Service CAVs moved on the battlefield.

"Cap'n," said Barse, "can we go back up the hill and pry open the beetle we foamed to death?"

"Why not? We deserve a look at them."

"They might suicide. That's what they did in space," said Liottey. He appeared pale and apprehensive at the notion of facing their enemy in spite of having defeated them decisively.

"Try to be a man, Gowan," Miza said. "I can't do it for the both of us. Not all the time."

Norlin let them argue as he returned to the hillside with the CAV tunnel bored through it. The aliens' black beetle had turned snowy white as the foam hardened.

"Reminds me of home during winter," Barse said wistfully. "Only there isn't a home anymore, thanks to them."

"Let's check it out." Norlin drove the CAV around the motionless alien craft then decided they had learned all they could from the safety of their armored vehicle. He and Barse climbed out and advanced slowly on the dead tank. Barse brushed sticky fire-suppression foam away from the air intakes for the turbines.

"They didn't design their vehicles too well. But then, these might not have been used before."

"Not on any world we know. I'll have to ask the admiral to send word to all frontier worlds and see how many respond. The Death Fleet's roster of successes has to be compiled."

"Some won't answer, no matter what you say," said Barse. "Murgatroyd wouldn't have. Rebel worlds are like that. Any hint of authority or being ordered and they back off."

Norlin said nothing to this. He knew the attitude and, deep down, increasingly approved of their independence. His contacts with the emperor's genhanced officers did not inspire confidence.

Facing this alien menace, however, was a war best fought united and not divided. The Death Fleet picked off each colony world with too much ease, unless they were opposed.

Sutton II had successfully defended itself, but at a tremendous cost. Norlin shuddered, thinking how few worlds had sector bases and the heavy armament to repel a space fleet. More would have to build their defenses. The word had to be spread. If it did, perhaps the Empire Service would not see so many mutinies.

Sutton's defense would have been far easier if so many Empire warships had remained in orbit, supported by the planet-based lasartillery.

"Here's the hatchway, Cap'n." Barse cycled it open. A fetid odor came out. "Something's dead inside and starting to turn ripe."

Norlin drew his pistol and made sure an explosive round chambered with a satisfying snick. Poking his head inside the dimly lit interior convinced him they had cut off all the power. The only illumination came from the sunlight.

"Lamp," he ordered. "I'm going in."

"Let Liottey risk his neck." Barse chuckled. "Let him earn another medal. That was clever of him to think of the foam."

"It'll soon be part of the permanent fighting system. Admiral Bendo is sharp enough to see the possibilities."

"It's so low-tech, though. It's almost offensively simple. Why, micron-diameter plastic spheres might work even better in getting through filters and gumming up turbines. They could be delivered by—hey, Cap'n, wait for me." Barse dived after him.

Norlin wiggled forward through a small tunnel until he came to the cockpit. He shined the lamp around and then laughed.

"What's so funny?" Barse pulled her short, stubby legs under her and looked around the aliens' cockpit. "Them? *They're* responsible for the Death Fleet?"

The two dead aliens were spider-limbed and barrel-chested, hardly the picture of invincible conquerors. Sharp beaks hung open, slack in death. Compound eyes stared at…what? Norlin wondered what their idea of an afterlife would be.

He also wondered what their philosophy of life was to despoil colonized worlds as they did. He wondered at a great deal more but was satisfied for the moment that they were dead.

"Bilateral symmetry, strangely jointed fingers, and it looks as if they have two thumbs. That'd make them experts at hitching rides. Brain case looks too big for the neck. The rest of the body I don't even want to think about. I wouldn't want to go on a bender and wake up the next morning with that beside me." She looked at the notch between the spindly legs and found nothing like human sexual organs.

"Chitin shell. They might be insectoid," said Norlin. He shook his head in disbelief. He had pictured the aliens to be towering brutes with prodigious muscles and impossible endurance.

On impulse, he reached out and took one frail arm and broke it over his knee. It was tougher than it looked, but not by much.

"Low-gravity world is my guess," said Barse.

"Let's get the hell out of here. The smell is making me sick. This is something for the admiral's research staff, not an engineer and a pilot."

"Yes, Cap'n, but we're one hell of an engineer and a damned fine pilot. That makes a difference."

Norlin took a deep breath when he got out of the alien fighting machine. He felt unclean. Those monsters had killed hundreds of millions of humans. They had been responsible for Neela's death, too. For that he could never forgive them.

He climbed to the top of the hill and stared into the dusty sunset. The sky turned dark, and the first stars appeared. He identified one and quickly worked his way to where the *Preceptor* orbited. It shone brighter than anything else in the twilight sky, as it should.

It was his ship.

And there was considerable work to do. The aliens' Death Fleet had shifted to another star system to destroy humans. They had to be found and stopped. He couldn't do it alone, but with Barse, Sarov, Miza and even Liottey aboard the *Preceptor* he could do much.

The alien Death Fleet would be stopped. Then they could find the aliens' home world and make certain Penum and Murgatroyd and Lyman never happened again. Pier Norlin made that promise to himself and humanity.

To be continued…

Afterword

Space opera. Blood and thunder. Thud and blunder along the spaceways. Excitement like it used to be.

That's what I tried to capture in the Star Frontiers trilogy, starting with this book, *Alien Death Fleet*. I grew up reading pulp fiction and have always had a soft spot in my heart for its conventions and moral certainty in its battles of good versus evil. Some might say this preference is a soft spot in the head, or "nostalgia idiotica," as SF author and fan writer Buck Coulson once called a longing to look back rather than forward.

So be it. I love space opera for the sweeping scope, the heroes who were heroes and heroines who were, well, heroines. EE "Doc" Smith smashed stars and galaxies together as heroes battled dastardly empires. Olaf Stapleton ranged from one end of time to another (and so did AE Van Vogt). Jack Williamson not only showed the Legion of Space but the Legion of Time to thrilling ends. Isaac Asimov built, destroyed and rebuilt galactic empires in his Foundation series. These are the grand stories of my youth and, stylistically lacking though they may be in light of today's deconstructionism, they soar because of concept.

Alien Death Fleet was originally sold to Pageant Books back in the late 1980s but, for legal reason having nothing to do with the book, was the only one of the three to see print. Zumaya Otherworlds reprinted this volume and published *Genetic Menace* and *Black Nebula*, completing the trilogy for the first time.

Consider these books a tribute to the science fiction's Golden Age. I hope you enjoy reading them as much as I did imagining them almost a quarter century ago.

Robert E. Vardeman

About the Author

ROBERT E. VARDEMAN is the author of nearly two hundred novels spanning many genres, but his favorites have always been science fiction and fantasy. He has served as vice-president of the Science Fiction Writers of America (SFWA) and also edited the organization's Forum. He is a member of the Western Writers of America (WWA) and the International Association of Media Tie-in Writers (IAMTW), serving as a judge for that organization's 2007 Scribe Award, and is also a member since its inception in 1979 of the informal group First Fridays, founded by mystery writer Tony Hillerman. For the past five years, he has worked on the editorial staff of four fantasy football magazines and is co-editor with Joan Saberhagen on the Baen Books anthology *Mask of the Sun: Golden Reflections*.

As a member of the Coalition for Excellence in Science Education, Vardeman served as consultant to the New Mexico State textbook advisory board in 2003.

About the Artist

BRAD W. FOSTER is an illustrator, cartoonist, writer, publisher, and whatever other labels he can use to get him through the door. He's won the Fan Artist Hugo a few times, picked up a Chesley Award and turned a bit of self-publishing started more than twenty-five years ago into the Jabberwocky Graphix publishing empire. (Total number of employees: 2.)

His strange drawings and cartoons have appeared in more than two thousand publications, half of those science fiction fanzines, where he draws just for the fun of it. On a more professional level, he has worked as an illustrator for various genre magazines and publishers, including *Amazing Stories* and *Dragon*. In comics, he had his own series some years back, *The Mechthings*, and he even got to play with the "big boys" for a few years as the official "Big Background Artist" of Image Comic's *Shadowhawk*.

His intricate pen-and-ink work has appeared in places as varied as *Cat Fancy, Cavalier*, and *Highlights for Children*, *Space & Time* and *Talebones*, and in illustrations for the first of Carole Nelson Douglas's Cozy Noir Press books featuring Midnight Louie.